THE TRUTH ABOUT MY Bat Mitzvah

by
NORA RALEIGH BASKIN

ALADDIN MIX
NEW YORK   LONDON   TORONTO   SYDNEY

ALADDIN MIX
Simon & Schuster Children's Publishing Division
1230 Avenue of the Americas, New York, NY 10020
Copyright © 2008 by Nora Raleigh Baskin
All rights reserved, including the right of reproduction in whole or in part in any form.
ALADDIN PAPERBACKS, ALADDIN MIX, and related logo are registered trademarks of Simon & Schuster, Inc.
Also available in a Simon & Schuster Books for Young Readers hardcover edition.
Designed by Lucy Ruth Cummins
The text of this book was set in Aldine.
Manufactured in the United States of America
First Aladdin Paperbacks edition April 2009
10 9 8 7 6 5 4 3
The Library of Congress has cataloged the hardcover edition as follows:
Baskin, Nora Raleigh.
The truth about my Bat Mitzvah / Nora Raleigh Baskin.—1st ed.
p. cm.
Summary: After her beloved grandmother, Nana, dies, nonreligious twelve-year-old Caroline becomes curious about her mother's Jewish ancestry.
ISBN-13: 978-1-4169-3558-2 (hc)   ISBN-10: 1-4169-3558-4 (hc)
1. Jews—United States—Juvenile fiction. [1. Jews—United States—Fiction. 2. Identity—Fiction. 3. Prejudices—Fiction. 4. Grandmothers—Fiction.] I. Title.
PZ7.B29233Tr 2008   [Fic]—dc22   2007001248
ISBN-13: 978-1-4169-7469-7 (pbk)   ISBN-10: 1-4169-7469-5 (pbk)
0912 OFF

FOR MY NANA

ACKNOWLEDGMENTS

This story would never have been drawn from my thoughts and memories and heart if it were not for Alexandra Cooper, my editor at Simon & Schuster. She then went on to coax it, plead with it, and sometimes gently force it into shape. Thank you.

Many thanks, once again, to my agent, Nancy Gallt, who seems to believe in me, even and especially when I don't.

And to Dal Lowenbein, who picks up the phone every time I call (up to ten times a day) to discuss a story idea, a character, and our children, our husbands, our dogs, or what I can possibly cook for dinner tonight. And she comes through every time.

And to all the people who have helped me with my own search for Jewish identity, Susan Cutler, Gail Abramowitz, Debbie Katchko, Charlene Monn, Annie and Batya Diamond, Stacy Kamisar, Anna Jo Dubow, Jill Becker, the Bi-Cultural Day School of Stamford, Connecticut, and of course, Rabbi Yehoshua and Freida Hecht.

AZ IKH VEL ZAYN VI ER, VER VET ZAYN VI IKH?
(IF I TRY TO BE LIKE HIM, WHO WILL BE LIKE ME?)

The Funeral

I was doing okay right up until I got to the doorway and saw her coffin. *My grandmother's body is inside there,* I thought, and I couldn't take another step into that room. I stopped short and my dad nearly bumped into me.

"Go on, Caroline," he said to me quietly. "Just walk inside and sit down."

Since we were the immediate family, we had been waiting in a special room. Everyone else, all my grandmother's friends and, I suppose, lesser family members, were already sitting out there, in seats like pews. Sitting, talking quietly. Everyone looked sad or at least serious. While we—my mom and dad and my little brother, Sam, my grandfather, and some old lady who I had never seen before—had been ushered in here. In this fancy room with the heavy furniture, oriental rugs, thick drapes, and pitchers of water with lemon, like we were special somehow. In a weird way it was like a birthday party, when you get treated differently for really no reason at all except that you were born—an event you personally had nothing to do with.

And now it was time for the service to start.

"I can't," I told my dad. My feet wouldn't move and I didn't know why.

My mom was still sitting in a big overstuffed chair in the corner of the waiting room, still crying. She had been crying all morning and on and off since we found out three days ago. It was her mother, after all, my nana. Even Sam was unusually quiet. Maybe he was just uncomfortable in his suit and tie.

My dad bent down and whispered into my ear, "Caroline, she's not really in there."

"What?" I turned to him and for a second I thought this whole thing had been a big mistake. We were in the wrong funeral home, the wrong place altogether. My grandmother didn't die. She wasn't inside that big, long box.

"Not really," my dad went on. "It's not her. Not the real Nana, not the Nana you remember. Don't be afraid. Just take the first step. I am right next to you."

And suddenly I could.

My feet started moving, one in front of the other. I followed my grandfather, with my dad beside me, my brother and mom holding hands, and then that old lady. We all made our way down to the front row, right in front of the coffin.

I sat down.

Everything after that was a blur. People got up and spoke but I didn't really listen to what they were saying. Especially not the rabbi who talked forever, even though he clearly had no idea

Nora Raleigh Baskin

who my grandmother was. Then he pronounced our names wrong. He mixed up my father and my uncle and he called me Carolyn instead of Caroline.

I looked over at my mom, who despised any kind of organized anything, religion in particular. She didn't even catch my glance as she normally would when she found something was false or insincere—and we would both roll our eyes knowingly. Now she was just crying.

I looked straight ahead and tried to remain calm. But the coffin was only a few feet in front of me. So close, I imagined I could *see* my nana, lying on her back with her hands folded the way they show it in the movies. Only this wasn't a movie and she really was in there, all closed up with a heavy wooden lid on top of her, so near to her face.

You know I can't go anywhere, my nana would always say, *until I put my face on.* She meant her makeup. My nana wouldn't leave her house without all her makeup on.

Then I started breathing really fast through my mouth and I felt dizzy. The tip of my nose was tingling. We would have to stand up soon. What if I fainted?

The thought of fainting made my heart beat really fast.

"Dad?" I whispered. My voice was shaking. Maybe I was going to throw up.

My dad took my hand in his and held it tightly.

"Remember, your nana's really not in there," he said again. "She'll always be with you." My dad took our two hands together and pressed them against my chest. "She'll always be in *here*," my dad said.

I put my other hand on top of his so he wouldn't take his hand away, not yet; I wasn't ready. I don't know if I believed him or not, but in a way it didn't matter. At least, I wasn't going to faint. I let out a slow breath. Then suddenly I started to cry. I would never see my nana again, and there had been so many things I didn't get to tell her.

Like how much I loved her.

I don't think I really ever let her know.

No, She Can't Be Related to Me

It seems like it shouldn't be, that you shouldn't get hungry when somebody dies, but you do. I was starving, actually, since none of us had had breakfast that morning. It was just all we could do to get into our best clothes without killing each other. My mother couldn't find a pair of stockings without a tear since she usually wears pants under her white hospital coat. Sam didn't have a real tie and he refused to wear a clip-on.

"I'm seven years old," he screamed.

My dad was upset that he didn't have any clean shirts from the cleaner. And I was pretty much left to my own devices, until I came downstairs dressed in pants.

"You can't wear that," my mother said. Her eyes were all red and puffy. She looked awful.

"Why not?" I asked. They were dressy khaki capris and I had on a nice top. I had worn the exact same outfit when we went to my cousin's graduation just a month ago.

"Because you can't."

I was going to argue but my dad gave me that look and I knew what it meant. So I went back upstairs and put on a long skirt and my platform sandals, which were pinching my feet. It was crowded here in my grandparents' apartment, which was filled with mostly older people who now seemed to have come alive. They were chatting and even laughing. I guess it was easy to forget why we were here and Nana wasn't. But not for me. Being in this apartment without her felt so wrong.

Even with all the mirrors draped in sheets. Even with the little cardboard boxes we were supposed to sit on, but nobody was. And even if it didn't feel right, I was still really hungry.

It had been hard to get close to the table laid out with cold cuts, pickles, olives, bagels, rye bread, and all sorts of spreads. And soda—I never get to drink soda. But I finally had a plate of food and a little plastic cup of ginger ale, when the old lady who had been in the waiting room at the funeral home came over and introduced herself to me.

"I'm your great-aunt Gertrude," the lady said. She held out her hand.

"My what?" I asked, and at the same time I found myself studying her face a little closer. An aunt? *Of mine?*

My grandfather suddenly stepped up.

"Caroline, this is my sister," Poppy explained. "My older sister, Gert. We haven't seen much of each other." Then he turned as if speaking only to her. "Not in a while . . . too long a while," he said.

I suppose it was possible I had relatives I didn't know about, but something told me there was more here, something more than the usual *Oh, it's been ages.*

Nora Raleigh Baskin

"Nice to meet you," I said. I gestured to the plate and cup filling both my hands as if she maybe hadn't noticed them before, but I had a feeling she was the kind of lady who usually got her way. She was tall, especially for an old lady, and her face was kind of droopy and mean looking.

"I am very sorry about your grandmother," she said, finally dropping her hand. "From what I hear, you two were very close."

I lowered my eyes at the mention of my nana. Something seemed odd about this whole situation.

"I hope to see you again very soon," my new aunt Gert said to me.

I was hoping not.

When everyone had left, it was just us: me and Mom and Dad, Sam and Poppy. Someone had been hired to clean everything up, so we had nothing to do but sit. For a long time no one said anything. Sam was about to fall asleep on my dad's shoulder.

My poppy sighed. "Amy, do you want to look at her jewelry?" He was talking to my mother.

She looked up. "What did you say, Dad?"

"Mom's jewelry," my poppy said. "Would you like to see if there is anything you want. To take home with you tonight."

"Oh no, Dad. Not now. I couldn't," my mother said.

I looked around. I could tell my grandfather needed to do something. He was a load-the-dishwasher, make-the-beds, go-to-work-at-the-same-time-every-day kind of guy. He wasn't very good at sitting around.

"I'll look," I offered.

My mother lifted her eyes to me.

"Just *look*," I said.

She nodded. She seemed too tired to move from her seat, but Poppy was already on his feet. I followed him into their bedroom. My grandparents had a giant bed. It was really two full-size beds pushed together with one headboard and one big bedspread over it. When I used to sleep between them I could feel the dip in the center, like lying in a cozy hammock. I would settle right into it and watch TV way later than my mother and father would ever let me at home.

My grandparents' bedroom smelled of her perfume. Nana always smelled like it, and so did everything she ever gave me, every sweater, every stuffed animal. It was from Paris, she once told me. *It is very expensive. Your poppy buys it for me once a year, every year since we were married.*

"The good stuff is in the bank," my grandfather told me. He sat down on the bed, taking my nana's jewelry box and setting it on his lap. "But there are some things in here that were meant for you one day."

"For me?"

He nodded.

"I don't want anything, Poppy," I said.

"I know you don't, sweetheart, but there is one thing I'd like to give you now."

"Now?"

My grandfather opened the top to reveal the two tiers of my nana's jewelry box. It was cushioned in satiny fabric, with separate compartments and tiny drawers. I had seen her take out her different earrings and big beaded necklaces many times before. I was never very interested in anything. Nothing in there was really to my taste. I didn't even have my ears pierced yet. My mother said I had to wait two more years, until I was fourteen, which seemed very unfair to me. I usually argued the point about once a month.

"Here," my grandfather said. He pulled out a necklace from one of the long rectangular compartments.

At first, all I could see was the gold chain, hundreds of miniature circles linked together. Then I saw it was a Star of David, a Jewish star: two elongated triangles, interlocked, one a slightly darker shade of gold than the other.

"She wanted you to have this," my poppy told me. "If you ever . . . you know."

"If I ever what, Poppy?"

"Well, it doesn't matter. It should be yours now."

He held the necklace up in the air, waiting, and when I lifted my hand he let it curl down into my open palm.

"You don't have to wear it," my grandfather said. "But just have it."

He pressed my fingers closed with one hand and brought his finger to his lips with the other. "Shhh. I don't have anything for Sam right now. But I want you to have this. It will make me feel better." He kissed my forehead.

"Okay," I said. Then we both sat there, like we didn't know what to do anymore. Like we were suddenly very tired.

I looked around the room, at her pillows, her framed needlepoint on the wall, her photographs on the dresser. I could feel the necklace inside my closed fist. There was her knitting bag, the needles poking out. Her shoeboxes stacked neatly in the closet. Nothing had changed. Her pocketbook was draped over the back of her vanity chair like she had put it there only moments before. It was as if my nana could walk into the bedroom any minute, or call me into the kitchen for the Chinese food we had ordered together.

Then I could, I *would*, tell her how much I loved the necklace. *It's so beautiful, Nana. Thank you.*

How Jewish Is Too Jewish?

I could tell my friend Rachel Miller anything. Even about what I heard in the car ride home when we finally left Poppy's apartment, when my parents thought I was asleep, like Sam was. Like I was, until we hit a bump on the West Side Highway. Through my lowered lashes, I saw my mother turn around in her seat to see if I had woken. It was late and dark, and the lights from the oncoming traffic shone into our car, making a kaleidoscope behind my lowered eyelids. I didn't even move my head. But I listened.

My mother went back to her conversation with my dad, in between crying. She was telling family secrets, and I wanted to hear them.

Rachel was my best friend, my best friend since nursery school. We were certain we had been separated at birth. For the first seven years of our friendship we looked exactly alike. In fact, it was because the other kids in our nursery school class couldn't tell us apart that Rachel and I met in the first place. Rachel went to the two-day-a-week fours program and I went to the three-day-a-week program, and the kids who went all five days a week thought we were the same little girl. They kept mixing up our names and calling Rachel Caroline and me Rachel. One kid got it all wrong and called us Racholine.

The teacher thought it was so funny, she insisted our moms meet each other. Our moms became best friends, and so did we. That was almost eight years ago, and we still use Carachel and Racholine for our screen names.

But lately, the last year or so, Rachel and I had stopped looking so much alike. To tell the truth, now I looked like Rachel's big sister. For one thing, Rachel's hair stayed golden blond, while mine was nearly totally dark brown now. And I had grown so much more; there was no hiding it, no amount of slouching. Sometimes, next to Rachel I felt like an elephant. But most times when I was with her, especially if we were alone, I'd forget. And we'd be like twins again, separated at birth.

We were both sitting on my bed, in my room. Rachel had come over first thing the next morning. She and her family had been at the funeral but they couldn't stay for the eating part, the shiva in my grandparent's apartment. Now I had so much to tell her.

"I heard them talking in the car," I told Rachel. "My mother and father on the way home last night when they thought I was sleeping. I found out why I never met my new aunt Gert before."

"Why?" Rachel asked.

"Well, I think my grandfather was mad at her," I began. I wasn't sure of the whole story myself. I wasn't sure who was still mad at who or who had done what when or for how long. It was confusing, and I was figuring it out myself, as I told it to Rachel.

"At who?" she asked.

"At his sister, the old lady who was sitting with us, remember? The kind of ugly lady?"

Rachel nodded. "So why?"

I tried to explain. "When my grandfather wanted to marry my grandmother, his whole family was against it. So against it, that my grandfather's father threatened to cut him off from the business and all their family money."

"They had family money? What's that mean?"

"I'm not sure . . . but I think my grandfather's family was really rich. They owned some big store in New York. You know, like Bloomingdale's . . . but not quite. They had been in America a long time. They lived on the Upper West Side of Manhattan, but my grandmother's family was still really poor."

I had already known that. Sometimes my nana would tell me stories about when she was little, but I never thought much of them. They were more like fairy tales, like *Hansel and Gretel* or *Sleeping Beauty*. Something you'd read in a book. Or see in a movie.

I went on. "So my grandmother's parents were both born in Europe somewhere so they still spoke Yiddish and kept kosher, stuff like that I guess. My grandfather's family told him if he married my nana, they would cut him off completely."

"But he married her anyway, didn't he?" Rachel said. "That's so romantic."

"Yeah, he did."

It was romantic, not that I could imagine my grandparents

that way. I could only see them in their big giant bed, with me in the middle. My nana doing her needlepoint, my poppy watching comedy shows on TV.

"I guess my nana's family was an embarrassment to my grandfather's family," I said. "They thought she was *too Jewish*. I heard my mother say that."

Rachel was Jewish. She was even having her bat mitzvah this year. So even though I did absolutely nothing Jewish at all, I liked that this little story connected us in a way. A little Jewishness between us, separated at birth.

At the same exact time but without saying so, we both lay back on my bed and looked up. A long time ago, my mom and I had cut circles from sticky shelf paper and stuck them on my ceiling. Now I had a solar system of purple and pink and red I could disappear into. I could float around and think about things without going too far.

"Can you believe that?" I asked Rachel. "*Too* Jewish."

"No," she said. "What does that mean? *Too* Jewish?"

I didn't know, but it made me think of the time Rachel's mom asked my mom if I was going to have a bat mitzvah. It was over a year ago. She was just starting to plan Rachel's—finding the right place, picking the date. She wanted to make sure there were no conflicts, that my family could all be there.

"We wouldn't miss it for the world," my mother said. "That's a great weekend for us."

That's when Rachel's mother asked, "Amy, do you ever think of having one for Caroline?"

They were having coffee while Rachel and I were working on a school project together in the other room.

Nora Raleigh Baskin

"Of course not," my mother answered.

I thought my mother said that a little too quickly. I had just happened to walk into the kitchen, looking for scissors. I decided to linger by the "everything drawer," where we kept everything we didn't know what else to do with. The scissors weren't supposed to be in there, since they *did* have a place, but they didn't happen to be in it at the time. I poked around and listened.

"Well, she *is* Jewish," Rachel's mom said. "Technically, since you're Jewish. I just thought you might have thought about a bat mitzvah for Caroline. Considered it."

"It would be hypocritical at this point," my mother said. "Besides, bar and bat mitzvahs have become so Americanized. Commercialized. With all the theme parties, the DJs and dancers."

I remember my mom had to call Rachel's mom that night and apologize.

Now Rachel and I lay on my bed and stared up into my ceiling, and in less than three months Rachel was going to have her bat mitzvah, or *become* a bat mitzvah, which was how she put it. She had a band and a caterer. She had invitations and yarmulkes with her name on them. Her whole family was coming; even her cousins from Israel were flying in.

We were best friends and Rachel had included me in everything and anything I wanted. I even helped her with the decision on the food for the kids' menu and the color of her tablecloths, lavender and navy blue. But then again, I didn't have to go to Hebrew school two days a week and on Sundays. I didn't have to learn a whole other language, and when Rachel showed me what she had to sing in Hebrew, I was so glad it wasn't me. At the same time, I kind of felt like maybe it should be me.

Or at least, it *could* be.

Nana, how could you be too Jewish when I am barely Jewish at all?

Nora Raleigh Baskin

I Would Have Been Nicer

Had I known my last visit with my grandmother was going to be my last, I think I would have been different. I would have tried to remember everything, set it in my brain, and held on to it.

I would have remembered to thank my grandmother for the terrific lunch at Gold's Deli because, for one thing, a chocolate egg cream is the most delicious drink in the whole wide world. It is sweet and milky and has the bite of soda all in one. The top is frothy and the bottom is thick with the unstirred syrup. And it comes in a big, tall glass, so full they bring it to you with a little plate underneath.

I would have asked her about her family. I would have listened better to her stories. I would have asked her about *her* mother. About her father, about where he was from. What did he do for a job? And what about all her brothers and sisters?

Maybe I would have asked her about Poppy.

When did they meet? How did they fall in love? Did she know about his family? How they disapproved? Did she know my new aunt Gert?

And after our lunch, after Poppy and Sam went back to the apartment and I went with Nana to her doctor's appointment, I wouldn't have done what I did. I never would have done what I did if I had known how sick she was.

Even though she told me later she wasn't mad at me.

I would never have hurt her feelings the way I did.

The appointment had taken a long time. It was hot in the waiting room and they had boring magazines. It was good to be in the fresh air, even if it was New York City. It was only a few blocks' walk back to my grandparents' apartment. My nana said it would do her good. She wanted to take my hand, but I didn't feel like it. I was a little jumpy. I looked up at the tall buildings, and at the sidewalk and all the people I didn't know.

And suddenly, I just wanted to try it out.

I wanted to walk without my grandmother in the streets of New York, on Lexington Avenue, so people would think I was by myself. I wanted to look like I was old enough to be alone. I wanted to see what it felt like to be a grown-up, just for a little bit, in a little way. So I stopped walking, quietly, before my nana could notice, and before I knew it she was almost a half a block ahead of me. For a second I got scared. She was too far away. What if she turned the corner and I couldn't see which way she went?

"Why are you back there, Caroline?" My nana turned and looked at me.

But I didn't even answer her.

I couldn't respond to a perfect stranger, could I?

"Caroline?" she called out again, and then, I guess, she gave up. I followed behind her, far enough to look like we weren't together at all.

Here I was, just walking by myself down the block. People passed me in both directions, couples and single woman, and a man walking his dog. Two teenagers smoking cigarettes. And me, Caroline Weeks, whoever that was.

Half and Half

In my house, we are both, I like to say. I'm half-Jewish, half-Christian, whenever someone asks. I guess to be honest it was a little more half and half when I was younger, when I first started nursery school and first met Rachel. We both went to the Jewish Community Center. Not because my mother wanted to introduce more religion into our lives. She didn't. My mother is not a big believer in things she cannot see or hear or prescribe medicine for.

My going to the JCC had more to do with how close it was to our house.

But we still had Christmas every year. My dad bought a tree and we hung stockings on the mantel by the fireplace. We had eggnog, which my mother said was too fattening but Sam and I loved. We left cookies for Santa, and we could barely sleep Christmas Eve.

But we also had Hanukkah. I made decorations in class at the JCC and my mother hung them up around the house. I learned what the letters on a dreidel meant. Of course, it helped when Hanukkah and Christmas came around the same time, but I remember one year when Hanukkah came right after Thanksgiving.

"It's tonight," I told my mother.

"No, it can't be," she said.

I was in public school by then. Rachel and I were in different classes that year, so it must have been second grade. There were only two Jewish kids in my room, Kate Nemerofsky and Danny Schiffman. They had been talking about it all day, talking about what presents they were getting. What they were going to eat. The teacher let them go to the front of the room and explain the Hanukkah story to the whole class.

I may have been only seven, but I still thought they were making way too big a deal out of it. Lighting candles and eating latkas—even spinning a dreidel was nothing compared to going to bed, too excited to even lie down, then somehow falling asleep, waking up way before you were supposed to, and running downstairs in your pajamas to a magical pile of presents that hadn't been there the night before.

But still, being half and half, I should have at least *known* it was Hanukkah.

"No, Mom." I insisted. "It's tonight. Tonight is the first night."

My mother is a doctor and she's not home a lot. She works all week and some weekends she's on call, so she's not home then, either. She works really hard and she saves people's lives, so I didn't blame her. Hanukkah just kind of crept up on us that year. She checked the Hadassah calendar we get every year because my parents give them money. I was right. It *was* tonight.

"Okay. Well, I'll get the menorah down from the attic," she said. But she looked tired. It was after eight o'clock and she had just gotten home from the hospital. She hadn't even eaten dinner yet.

"It's okay, Mom. There are seven more nights," I said.

Sam was just a baby then. He didn't even notice. I think we lit the menorah three, maybe four nights that year, and that's probably when Hanukkah started to peter out in our house. Half and half became seventy-five/twenty-five. Then more like eighty/twenty.

But the truth was, what I had really meant to say was, *It's okay, Mom. There's seven more nights. As long as you don't forget Christmas.*

But how *could* anyone forget Christmas?

It was all around us, everywhere, and it began early. The local stores had red and green decorations up so early, it was almost as if they had never come down from the year before. TV commercials with Santa Claus and Christmas trees started pretty much right after Halloween. At the grocery store and the pharmacy and everywhere you went, people said "Merry Christmas" instead of good-bye. So if you didn't want to correct everyone every time, you just got used to it.

The principal at our school played holiday music over the announcements in the morning for the entire month of December. They weren't religious, but everyone knew they were Christmas songs. The tinsel was so sparkly and the lights were so pretty. My favorites were the houses with one single white light in every window.

But most of all, *everyone* celebrated it, talked about it, waited for it.

Nora Raleigh Baskin

Everyone except Kate Nemerofsky. Danny Schiffman.

And my best friend, Rachel Miller, who not only celebrated Hanukkah but also Passover, and Rosh Hashanah, and some other holidays I didn't know anything about.

It's My Birthright to Play Hooky

Tomorrow, according to Rachel, is Yom Kippur.

I found out this particular bit of information on the phone. I wanted to borrow a book she had for a report I needed to do in social studies.

"Sorry, Caroline. I'm not going to school tomorrow," Rachel told me.

"You're not?"

"No, remember? I told you. It's a holiday."

"Oh, right," I said.

But hadn't there been a Jewish holiday just last week? While I was still on the phone with Rachel, I was already imagining her empty chair in homeroom. And then I suppose, Danny and Kate would be absent from math and English, respectively. Because they were Jewish too.

But so was I, wasn't I?

Rachel's mother said I was Jewish because my mother was

Jewish, and my mother was Jewish because my grandmother was, my nana. I suspected that went on and on, backward, for a very long time. And so just because my mother was throwing the whole thing away didn't mean I wanted to.

Besides, I could use a day off from school.

We were having a chapter test in math.

Thinking about my grandmother still hurt, like a sharp pain in my throat I had to will away if I didn't want to cry. Sometimes it would come to me like a sense, like a memory—not of her, exactly, but the feel of her hugging me or taking my hand. The smell of her perfume, hanging in the air.

"I won't even be able to call you afterward," Rachel was telling me on the phone. "We have to drive out to New Jersey to eat. We won't be back till late."

"Okay. Well, have fun," I said, which sounded so lame but I didn't know what else to say. I had no idea what Yom Kippur was or what you were supposed to do, but I felt stupid asking Rachel. I didn't want her to know how much I really didn't know.

I didn't sleep well that night, which turned out to be the best thing because I looked terrible in the morning.

"What do you mean, you're not feeling well?" my dad was asking me.

My mother had already left for work. It was Wednesday, so she had early office hours. My dad was putting out cereal and juice. He was already showered and ready to drive Sam to school and head to work himself. He and his partner, Jason, owned a promotional advertising company. They were the ones who thought up those giveaways and contests you see on the inside of bottletops and on bags of chips.

"You do look pretty bad," Sam said. He was practically standing on his chair, leaning half his body over the table and reaching for the box of Cheerios.

"I think I'm sick," I said.

Wednesday was our busiest morning, so I knew my dad would give in pretty quickly. The more stressed he was, the easier this would be. That's when Sam tipped over his entire glass of orange juice.

I couldn't have planned it better.

"Oh, Sam," my dad said.

"Sorry," my brother said. He slid down from his chair. "Sorry, Daddy."

"I'll get it," I said. "You get yourself ready, Dad. Take Sammy to school. I got this."

My dad was about to thank me profusely but stopped when he looked up and saw me. "Caroline, you're still in your pajamas. The bus comes in"—he looked at his watch—"five minutes."

"Dad, I think I have a fever."

That was a mistake.

"A fever?"

"I mean, I'm fine. I'll be fine," I said. I started sopping up the juice with a paper napkin, with three paper napkins. If my mother were here, she'd tell me to get a sponge, but my dad didn't notice. "I just need a rest, a little rest today," I said.

My dad paused for a moment, like he was frozen, thinking. It was probably a combination of worrying about me not feeling well, trying to remember how old I was and if I could be left home alone, and wondering what would mom do in this situation.

　　　　　　　　　　　　　　　　　　　Nora Raleigh Baskin

"Dad, I'm almost thirteen," I said.

"Yeah, Dad," Sam added. "She's practically a whole grown-up. She's even got little boobies."

My dad looked at Sam and then to me, and then quickly back to Sam.

But that had done the trick.

I was off for the day.

Oh, Yeah, She Must Be Jewish

I sat outside after watching back-to-back episodes of *Real World* that I had already seen before, and two hours of the Game Show Channel. The leaves were only beginning to turn colors. They brushed against one another in the wind, just the tiniest bit louder, the tiniest bit closer to drying out, turning brown, and falling to the ground. I let the sun touch my face.

So this is Yom Kippur?

I wondered what Rachel was doing at this moment, but I really had no idea other than that she was going to New Jersey to eat. Funny that I never asked her. I never thought about it before. Did my grandparents in New York do anything on this day? Did everybody that was Jewish know what to do?

I had lost track of time but it was probably after one o'clock. I would be in gym right now. We were square dancing this semester, to coincide with our colonial unit in social studies. I can't say I liked square dancing, but it was better than volleyball and I was pretty good at it. And best yet, the last two classes, Mrs. Danower had used me for her demonstration.

Me and Ryan Berk, who for years had ridden my bus, but I'd never noticed him before that first class.

We had to do-si-do and then do a quick promenade. Ryan's grip was a little sweaty but I didn't mind. I tried to make it look like my hand was just passing by my leg—I didn't want him to see me wipe my hand off on my jeans as we walked back to our group.

"Now do-si-do and allemande your partner," Mrs. Danower shouted out. Everyone started moving at once in their circle, turning the wrong way and bumping into each other. Only Ryan and I had it right. It wasn't exactly *Dancing with the Stars* but it was pretty cool.

Ryan didn't look at me while we were dancing. He looked just about everywhere else, but the next gym class, he asked if I wanted to be his partner again.

I realized I kind of had two lies going today. One, that I was sick, and two, that I was Jewish, but if I sat here on my porch steps any longer I'd get a tan, and that would be hard to explain either way.

Still, I didn't want to move. I closed my eyes, wondering if I cared whether or not Ryan Berk liked me.

Liked me *that* way.

I went inside, into my bedroom, and took out the necklace my grandfather had given me. Maybe if I put it on, something Jewish would come to me. I had wrapped it in tissue and stuck it in the corner of my top dresser drawer. No one at school was going to notice I wasn't there anyway. And if they did, it's not like they were going to wonder if I was absent because I was celebrating Yom Kippur. Is that the right word? Do people *celebrate* Yom Kippur? I didn't even know.

It's not like they were going to think, *Oh, yeah. Caroline Weeks isn't here today. She must be Jewish.*

I pushed my top drawer closed without taking out the necklace. Maybe I should have gone to school. If I hadn't stayed home, I could be half sashaying with Ryan Berk right at this very moment.

This whole skipping school was a stupid idea. I was stupid. And worse, I was bored.

I was so bored I lay on my bed and fell asleep.

Everyone Needs Something to Hold On To

You know when you fall asleep but you're not really tired because it's the middle of the day? You just fall asleep because there's nothing else to do.

And you start to dream but you *know* you're dreaming?

That's what happened to me.

I am swimming.

Swimming and swimming but not getting anywhere, like my legs are stuck in mud, or tangled, twisted in the blankets. Now I am in the deep ocean and I am pretty far out from shore, too far. And when I realize I am not getting anywhere no matter how hard I paddle and move my arms around, I begin to panic. I am terrified, desperate for something to grab on to.

I am flailing my arms around but there is no one.

I am going to drown. My body is like lead. I can feel the water on my face.

I can feel tears springing into my eyes. I am so scared. I want a ladder, a rope. Something to grab on to. Someone to reach out, pull me in. I can feel the water in my nose.

Then suddenly I am not drowning.

I'm crying. I am crying and crying, half-asleep and half-awake. I can feel the wetness on my pillow and my mind is telling me to wake up. I am only dreaming. *It's the middle of the afternoon,* I tell myself.

Wake up. Wake up. Open your eyes.

I try to will myself awake. I force my eyes open.

Open.

Now there is no ocean. No water. *It's Wednesday, remember? Square dancing. I skipped school, remember?*

I am home sick.

And I'm probably going to get in trouble for skipping school, but a part of me is just so relieved not to be drowning. Then just before I wake up completely, I think I feel my grandmother with me. It is so real and so strong. And it's not just the awareness, it's the feeling of being loved. Of being a part of someone, connected without touching. Like perfume lingering in the air.

Nana? I whisper. And then just like that, it is gone.

But not entirely.

The Zelkowitz Affair

Really, the most Jewish thing I'd ever done was lighting a candle at a bar mitzvah. And ironically, it was my dad's friend. It was the bar mitzvah of his business partner's son, Matthew Zelkowitz.

We had known them for years. We had Thanksgiving with them a few times. We even went away with them on vacations when Sam and I were younger, when the year's difference between me and Matthew, and the two years between Sammy and Matt's little sister, Brittney, didn't matter. We didn't see them as much anymore but we knew our whole family would be invited to his bar mitzvah.

Still, nobody warned us this was going to happen, that we were going to be called up—to the tune of "You've Got to Have Friends"—to light a candle. My family and I were just minding our own business, sitting at our seats.

Not that finding our seats had been an easy thing to do. All the place cards were set up on a table outside the main room of the hotel in alphabetical order and there were hundreds of them, perfectly lined up paper pup tents. After an hour of what I thought was the main meal but turned out to be appetizers, a woman in a tuxedo wandered around with a little bell and told everyone to go inside and find their seats.

"What does this mean?" Sammy said. He had found our names and grabbed the cards right off the table, sending the neat, straight rows into jagged disorder, but it didn't matter because pretty much right after he did that, everyone started grabbing for theirs.

"What?" my dad asked.

Sammy had three place cards in his hands. He was reading the inside of his.

"Water Works," he read. "What does that mean?"

I took my card from my brother's hand and opened it up. "Electric company," I said out loud.

I didn't know anyone at this party. I knew my dad's partner, Jason, and his wife, Marcia. And I knew their kids, Matthew and Brittney, but not very well anymore and certainly not *their* friends, so I had been forced to hang out with my parents and my little brother. The service had been long and mostly in Hebrew. People stood up and sat down constantly and there was a lot of singing. I looked over at my mom to see if she knew the words. Her lips never opened.

"We are on Tennessee Avenue," my dad announced when he read his place card. "My favorite."

"Oh, it's Monopoly!" Sam said suddenly, very pleased with himself.

"Monopoly what?" I asked.

My mother folded her card and slipped it into the jacket of her suit. "It's the theme," she explained. Then she looked at me. "Don't ask," she said, rolling her eyes.

When we walked into the party room, I understood. Every table had a sign on it, a blowup of a property on the Monopoly game board. There was New York Avenue in orange, St. Charles Place in purple. Vermont Avenue was light blue, Atlantic and Ventnor, yellow. That's when I realized we weren't sitting together. The grown-ups had street properties; the kids must have the utilities. I wasn't even sitting with Sam.

"Mom?" I looked at her. My dad was good with sensitive things, but my mom was better at negotiations. My dad would tell me I could handle it. My mom would move chairs around.

The music was blasting as we looked around for our table. There was a full band on a large platform toward one end of the room, with a woman singer in a long slinky dress crooning into her microphone. But there was also what looked like a DJ setup and four or five young men and women dressed in black-and-gold spandex moving slowly to the music, as if they were not quite yet aware of all the guests now pouring into the room. It took me a moment to realize they were entertainers, just waiting to perform.

All around the room huge television sets were suspended from the ceiling. They hung down at an angle, and I just realized, it was so you could watch the whole party. As it was happening!

Sure enough, my mom managed to get us all sitting at the same table. She explained to one of the thousand waiters standing around that her children would prefer to sit with their parents than at either the kids' table or the teenagers' table, and within half a minute new chairs and place settings were arranged.

Now we were all sitting together on Tennessee Avenue. Mr. Monopoly, with his shiny top hat and handlebar moustache greeted us. Beside each salad plate was a miniature canvas bag, tied at the top and stamped with a money sign.

Sammy already had his opened and was counting the fake bills inside.

"Don't, Sam. You're not supposed to touch that," I said to him.

"I can. Why not?" But he wasn't sure. He looked around to see if anyone else was opening their bag of money.

"It's okay," I told Sam.

I think the sensory overload was getting to me. The music was loud. There were too many people, too much movement, too many plates and pieces of silverware and glasses at the table. Instead of a centerpiece of flowers like I had seen before at weddings, there was a huge crystal bowl in the middle of the table. It was stuffed with what looked like, yes . . . over-size Chance cards and giant Community Chest cards, and sticking out of the top were all the different Monopoly tokens. Not the little metal ones that come with the game but large replicas made of plastic or Styrofoam. The terrier, the top hat, the shoe, the wheelbarrow, the race car. They were all there, and as I looked around me, every table had the same thing.

A bunch of the kids were gathered around the back of the room, and I figured out there were blackjack tables set up there. Against the wall was a giant roulette wheel. Sammy did some scouting and reported back to me.

"They have a guy who will take your picture and put it on the

Nora Raleigh Baskin

cover of any magazine you want. Like *People*. Or *Time*. Or *Sports Illustrated*."

"No, thanks," I said.

Matthew Zelkowitz didn't look anything like a man to me. He didn't look much older than my brother, but I knew he was. Still, he had stood on the stage in the synagogue and nearly without crying recited a very long song in Hebrew.

Now he was standing in the front of this whole crowd of guests, a complete orchestra all quietly holding their instruments, the dancers, the hip-hop DJ, the really tall MC with the big mouth (who had somehow silenced the entire room), an enormous waitstaff looking bored but ready, and three separate photographers (one standing on a ladder) and one video guy.

Someone handed Matthew his own microphone. Someone else wheeled out a table with a huge, flat birthday cake, its entire perimeter staked out with tall, skinny white candles. One by one he called up his family and close friends to light them. It took me a while to figure out that the DJ played a different song each time, something that related to the guest who had been called up. It was pretty cool. The cake was nearly on fire by the time he got to candle number eleven.

"It may be business but you've been like family. Sammy, Caroline, Amy, and Randall—come on up and light my eleventh candle!"

That was us!

It was my family. My dad and mom, and even me and Sammy. We all sat looking at one another for a moment. Then I saw my mom had this big smile on her face. My dad, too. They stood up and motioned for us to do the same. Watching everyone else go up there and stand next to Matthew had been fun, but this was exciting. I remember thinking this is really important, an honor. He had chosen my dad and us because we meant something to him. Because we had shared memories and we were connected no matter how old we got or how little we might see one another. Because he cared about us.

In the picture that Marcia Zelkowitz sent us a couple of months later I am smiling so big I think my cheeks will split.

Girls Like Who?

I was right about Yom Kippur. Nobody at school put it together. Nobody came up to me and said, "Oh, cool, Caroline, I didn't know you were Jewish." Rachel didn't even ask, because, of course, she didn't know I wasn't in school yesterday.

I didn't feel like bringing it up to her. I felt silly. It was Thursday. I'd missed a math test, that's all, and now I had to make it up before the end of the week. Nothing had changed for me, but apparently Ryan had found a new square-dancing part-ner in my absence because *she* came up and told me about it.

"Oh, hey, Caroline. We missed you in gym yesterday. But it's okay. I filled in for you."

It was the new girl, Lauren Chase. Rachel and I still called her "the new girl" even though she had been here since the end of sixth grade last year. She showed up around April as the new girl from Virginia. Richmond, Virginia. She was in my science class this year, which is where I was headed right now.

"We did a lot of square dancing at my old school," Lauren informed me.

I responded with my old tried and true, "What was that?" which is meant to buy time until I can think of something more clever but never works. So I suppose, in reality, it is only tried but not true.

Lauren laughed, showing her white teeth. She did that a lot. "It was fun. Ryan's got really nice moves," she said.

Nice moves?

Who says something like that? Maybe you just need the Southern accent to pull it off. Lauren walked into the science room ahead of me.

No, I thought. "Nice moves" sounded stupid any way you said it.

I followed her in.

Then just as class was about to start, Lauren leaned as far over her desk as possible. "Hey, Caroline. By the way, I'm having a sleepover in two weeks. For my birthday. Do you want to come?"

Now, Lauren was one of those popularity enigmas. Most of us had to pay our dues. We had to suffer through second-tier seating in the cafeteria, last-place picks for gym teams, and a lack of invitations to certain "popular girl" birthday parties. It was work just to get a halfway decent status position in the middle school—not at the top, but not at the very bottom, either.

But Lauren Chase had somehow skipped all those steps.

She came onto the scene popular.

Like being praised by Simon Cowell on your first song.

I think it was her blond hair. Her clothes, certainly. And the way she just assumed it. I believe I am popular, therefore I am, and therefore everyone else will believe it as well. As much as I didn't like her, I wanted so badly to be just like her.

"Well, do you?" Lauren asked again.

I wanted to know if Rachel Miller was invited too. I wanted to tell her I'd get back to her when I found out. Because I wouldn't go to any party Rachel wasn't invited to.

Really, I wanted to know why she was inviting me at all.

Did she think I was someone else? I was trying to remember if she had called me by my name or not.

"Look, if you don't want to . . . ," Lauren pressed.

"No, I do."

Then I crossed my legs casually and looked up like I was waiting for the teacher to start class, which I really wasn't since I just remembered I hadn't done the homework. "Thanks," I added, to seal the deal before it was off the table.

Lauren whipped her hair around off her shoulders and leaned back against her seat. "Good," she said.

At lunch, I was anxious about telling Rachel about Lauren's invitation.

I waited until we were both sitting down with our lunch trays. It was noisy and crowded and the hot lunch looked awful. I picked at my Beefaroni with my plastic fork while I thought of the right way to phrase what I wanted to say. I knew Rachel's feelings would be hurt if she hadn't been invited to Lauren's party and I was. But if Lauren had asked her, too, then Rachel was probably just as worried about telling me. I needed to say it just right, slowly. . . .

"So Lauren Chase just invited me to her sleepover party," I finally just blurted out.

"Oh." Rachel looked up and smiled at me. "I'm so glad," she said. "I got an invitation too and I was so worried that you didn't. But now we can both go. Right? I mean, if we want to."

"Yeah, I guess. Do we want to? We don't even like her. Do we?"

"No. But oh, who cares." Rachel laughed. "Maybe it will be fun."

We talked about who else would probably be going, what we would wear. And could Rachel borrow my brother's sleeping bag if we needed to bring our own.

Of course.

I was so excited that we had both been invited, it wasn't until after we finished lunch, brought up our trays, and had each headed off to our fifth-period class that I realized something.

Had Rachel said she got an invitation?

Like a paper one? In the mail? But Lauren had just told me about it in school, just a few minutes ago. So maybe *I* was the afterthought. Maybe someone else couldn't come to Lauren's party and I was just a fill-in.

I was trying to figure it all out as I got on the bus and took my seat next to Megan Nichols. Maybe Lauren didn't want to invite me but she was trying to get in closer with Ryan Berk. Maybe she *liked* him?

"Hi, Caroline," Megan said.

Well, there was nothing I could do about it anyway.

"Hi, Megan." I smiled.

Megan was my school-bus friend. She wasn't in any of my classes but I really liked her. In school, Megan hardly talked to anyone, and I suppose that was part of the reason she was near the bottom of the middle school social ladder, but I think it had

Nora Raleigh Baskin

more to do with her clothes (Megan made *me* look like a fashion model), and maybe how shy she was.

A girl like Lauren would never invite someone like Megan Nichols to her party. I was just lucky to be invited at all.

What's a Knish?

"Glad you're feeling better today," my mom said to me that night. She was sitting at the end of my bed.

At first I didn't even know what she meant. How could she know about Lauren Chase's birthday party? No, of course she couldn't. She was talking about yesterday. About Wednesday, about skipping school.

"Oh, yeah. I am," I said, even though I already knew she knew.

What chance did I have? I mean, my mom's a doctor. I was caught. I was just not sure of what. For pretending to be Jewish, or for playing hooky? I was getting my big excuse story all ready, but I didn't need it.

When I looked at my mother, I saw her eyes were filling.

I knew this wasn't about my missing school. She had cried so much these last weeks, since Nana died. She turned her head but I saw that she was trying to bat her tears away, blinking her eyes like crazy.

"Hey," my mother said suddenly. "Do you want to go with me Sunday? Into the city to help Poppy. I think he's probably going to move to Florida year-round soon. Not just fall and winter. Retirement, you know. And Aunt Gert has a place down there too."

My mother's face is so pretty. If I had to pick a movie star that she looked like, it would be Amy Irving, Steven Spielberg's first wife, and not just because my mother's name is Amy too. It would be because of her hair, mostly, I suppose. My mother's hair curls in ringlets, golden brown ringlets. Her face is round, like a soft heart.

Her eyes are light brown, like mine.

"Okay," I said. I was lying down with my head on my pillow. "I'll go with you."

She smiled. Her eyes were dry now. "Want me to tuck you in?" she asked.

I hadn't been *tucked in* in a long time. "Okay."

There isn't much to the ritual. Really, it isn't anything more than pulling the covers up to my chin and then patting them down around my body, my feet, and up to my shoulders. I never liked my covers tucked under the mattress. My legs like a little "elbow room" so I can shift around while I get comfortable without pulling out my blankets. My mother knew how to do it just right, so I was tucked in but not confined. Comfortable but not trapped.

Then she always used to say the same thing: *Tight as a knish.*

Only she pronounces it like its two syllables, almost. *K-nish*, but not exactly. When I was little, I used to wait till she left the room, then I would practice saying it in the dark to myself.

Kenish. Nish. Kinish. K-nish.

But what is a knish? Something to wear? Something to eat? I just knew it was something Jewish, like *shayna maideleh* and *oiy vey*; something Nana probably said to my mother when she was a little girl.

I just never thought to ask.

"Tight as a knish," my mother said now, but she didn't turn off my light. She stood in my doorway with her hand on the switch. "Caroline, start thinking of something you might like. Something of Nana's."

I guess I could have told my mother about the necklace right then, but I was afraid she'd think it was silly. Or she'd say something like she said to Rachel's mother, that it was hypocritical, like having a bat mitzvah.

"Okay, sweetie? Something to remember her by. Maybe one of her needlepoint pictures or one of those little figurines she collected."

She flipped off my light.

"Okay, Mom," I said into the darkness, but I didn't have to think.

I knew exactly what I wanted.

Putting on Her Face

The first time I ever got to see my nana without her makeup on, I was five years old. I will never forget it. It was the first time I got to sleep at my grandparents' apartment by myself. Sam wasn't even born yet.

I was taking my bath in the tub in the morning, even though at home I took my bath at night. I remember how I loved the black and white tiles in their tiny bathroom, the matching towels, and the fuzzy cover on the toilet seat.

"Can I come in?" My grandmother knocked on the door. She was already in.

"Sure, Nana," I said.

My grandmother was still in her underwear and I think I was more embarrassed than she was. She looked like she was outfitted in white armor, a big, huge bra and massive underwear combined into one, only her arms and legs sticking out. I couldn't imagine how she had gotten herself into it. But she had.

"You know we can't go anywhere until I put on my face." She always said that. She had to "put on her face." Without her make-up my nana was like a completely different person. Her lips were faded and thinner, her eyes were smaller, and her eyebrows were totally nonexistent. But I thought she looked much more beautiful.

I remember thinking, I could see more of her.

The very first thing my nana did was take a small round cotton ball and press it to the top of her favorite, her only, perfume bottle. The room filled with the sweet smell. She flipped the bottle over once, quickly, and then she tucked the damp cotton ball into her bra, right between her breasts.

Then she continued to talk to me while she was blotting her face with what looked like squares of tissue paper, up and down, all over her skin.

"Did you have a good night's sleep?"

"Of course," I answered. I lowered my back into the hot water. My legs stretched out and my feet rose up, not quite touching the shiny metal faucet.

"Was it too noisy last night for you?" she asked. "It can be so noisy in the city and you are a country girl."

"I live in Greenport, Connecticut, Nana, and I slept good," I answered.

Because I loved the sounds of the cars beeping, the mournful sirens, the sharp voices that would drift up from Lexington avenue all night long. It was comforting to me. It was Nana and Poppy's apartment. It felt warm and safe. I felt like I belonged here.

"Now for the most important step," my grandmother said. I had to poke my head out of the curtain again to see.

Nora Raleigh Baskin

"Moisturize," she said. She rubbed her whole face with cream, till she shone.

While I watched, I was hoping we would order Chinese food that night, even though we hadn't had breakfast yet. I would get egg rolls. Wonton soup. Fried rice. Lo mein. Maybe sweet and sour chicken. But I didn't have to worry. We always got Chinese food when we came to my grandparents' apartment.

Nana was in the middle of spreading the liquid foundation that made her look tan. She never missed a spot, and you would never see that line some old ladies get all along their jaw. That line that makes you wonder if they were blind when they were putting on their makeup, or when they asked, "Do I look all right?" that someone was playing a nasty joke on them. Never my grandmother.

"What would you like for dinner, my *shayna maideleh*?" my nana asked. I remember thinking that she could read my mind.

Shayna maideleh? She had probably said it a hundred times before, but it was the first time I really heard it. Now she was putting on her eyes, a liquid black line on the top and on the bottom. Fake eyelashes and then blue shadow.

"What does that mean?" I asked her.

"What does what mean?" Nana was leaning in toward the mirror, drawing eyebrows, perfect arches where they must have once, long ago, grown all by themselves.

"What you called me. Shayna you-know-what."

She turned to me, her face was almost completely on. "*Shayna maideleh*? It means my pretty girl. Caroline, my beautiful granddaughter. My *shayna maideleh*. In Yiddish."

"Did you used to call my mother that?" I asked her.

"Of course I did," she told me. "All the time."

The last thing my nana did, I noticed, was her lips. She took a colored pencil and drew a line just outside where her lips really were, and then filled it in with red lipstick. While I watched she reached over and tore off a single sheet of toilet paper. She pressed it to her lips and then tossed it away.

"I'm going to get dressed now. You take as long as you want. So how about Chinese food for a change?"

"That's a funny one, Nana."

She shut the door behind her.

When I was getting out of the tub, drying myself with a big soft towel, I looked down into the wicker trash basket under the sink, and there was my nana's fragile red kiss.

Now I wish I had thought to take it out and save it.

Nora Raleigh Baskin

13

Who Will Be Like Me?

It was called Hermès Calèche, straight from Paris. Nana's perfume.

That was the one thing I wanted.

My mother said I had to keep it from the sun or the liquid inside would evaporate. It would happen eventually, she told me, but it would take a very long time if I kept it safe. And the scent would just get stronger in the meantime.

As soon as I got home from New York City, I went into my room, shut my door, and slid my desk chair in front to block it, just in case. I opened my nana's bottle of perfume and held it to my nose. Suddenly it was like she was in the room with me. Or like she had just passed through and she'd be back in a minute.

Only I knew she wouldn't be. That was a hollow feeling I could barely stand.

I reached inside my drawer and felt around for the tissue

paper. I took out my necklace and clasped it around my neck and I looked at myself in the mirror above my dresser.

About a year ago, Rachel and I wanted to go to the mall. We wanted to go by ourselves and we had prepared a list of five or six girls in our grade that had already done so without being killed or kidnapped. But our mothers were united and neither one would allow it. They had to go with us.

"We won't even talk to you," Rachel's mother said. "Promise."

"I swear, we'll walk seven paces behind you at all times," my mother added.

They were making fun of us.

"We'll pretend we don't even know you."

"We'll pretend we don't even *like* you."

They died laughing but it was really annoying, and of course they didn't keep any of their promises. They talked to us the whole time and commented on everything we looked at. And then we went into Claire's to look at the jewelry. Our mothers had temporarily slipped away behind some feather boas and studded leather belts.

"These are nice." Rachel was spinning one of the tall rotating displays of earrings.

"Oh, I love this," I said. I was looking at a crystal. I suppose it wasn't real crystal since it was only a twelve-dollar necklace, but the rose-colored, cut surfaces sparkled like a diamond's, a crystal cross shape on a black rope.

"Try it on," Rachel said from behind the earring display. "Let me see."

I stepped around to stand in front of her and show her what I was wearing.

"Oh," she said. "It's a cross."

"So? Isn't it pretty?" It lay just below my collarbone and was the exact hue of the shirt I happened to be wearing. "It's cool. It doesn't mean anything. I mean, it doesn't have to."

"But it does," Rachel said.

I shrugged and hung the necklace back up where I had gotten it from.

Now I put my fingers up to my throat and touched the pointy Star of David, my grandmother's necklace, a delicate chain made up of countless tiny links. If I wear this, will people think I am Jewish?

Is that what I want to be?

Will I be?

Now If *I* Were Having a Bat Mitzvah

"Do you think I have to invite Lauren now?" Rachel was asking me.

"To your bat mitzvah? Lauren Chase?"

Rachel and I were in our after-school program art class, working on our charcoal still lifes. Lauren's sleepover birthday party was less than a week away. I still hadn't had the guts to ask Rachel if she had received an invitation in the mail or an informal verbal one like me. I decided it didn't matter; we were both going to our first A-list sleepover.

I wasn't sure I really wanted to go, but it was better than not having been invited at all.

But Lauren Chase at Rachel's bat mitzvah!

"Why?" I asked Rachel. "It would throw the whole balance off. We had it all figured out."

The more I thought about it, the worse it was beginning to sound.

"Well, my mom said I should," Rachel admitted. She hadn't even begun her drawing. In the center of the room on a little table sat a blue-striped bowl with one pineapple, three apples, and a bunch of grapes that hung over the side like they were trying to escape. One pear stood on the table, outside the bowl, left out or already freed. It was hard to tell.

"She said if I wanted to go to Lauren's sleepover I should want Lauren to come to my party."

"But a birthday isn't anything like a bat mitzvah," I practically shouted.

The image of Lauren's long blond hair and expensive dress, strappy shoes, and stuck-up attitude was ruining Rachel's special day for me already. We had put so much thought into who to invite.

We had started with one huge, long list of nearly everyone we knew. Rachel's mom had given her a number: sixteen, eight girls and eight boys. Not including family friends who had kids, not including business friends who had kids, not including family, like cousins. Sixteen kids who were just Rachel's choice.

"Does that mean me?" I asked. "Am I one of the eight girls?"

We were in Rachel's bedroom with a notebook.

"No," Rachel told me. "You are a family-friend kid. We can invite eight other girls *besides* us two."

"And eight boys," I added. This was way before Ryan Berk asked me to square-dance.

It was exciting, powerful, even. It was going to be a big deal. All the girls would wear dresses and the boys would have to wear suits or at least jackets and nice pants. My mother had promised me we could go into New York City to shop for a special dress just for Rachel's bat mitzvah.

Rachel started shaping a pineapple and the bumps of what I thought were going to be the grapes with her stick of charcoal. "My mom said I shouldn't go to Lauren's party if I didn't want to invite her to mine."

"What are we going to do?"

"Invite her, I guess. My invitations haven't gone out yet. I still could. She'd never know she wasn't on our original list. It wouldn't hurt her feelings."

"But we don't even like her!" My hands were black with charcoal. I wasn't paying attention to my picture and I was smearing what I had done with the sleeve of my shirt. Not to mention getting my sleeve dirty.

"You forgot your smock again, Caroline." Mrs. Fein walked by. "Very nice drawing, though. Very nice."

I looked down at my paper. The smear had created a kind of shadowy third dimension I didn't know I could draw.

"And nice start, Rachel. Try to hurry a little. Class is almost over."

I thought the teachers who taught afterschool programs were always nicer than during the regular day because they knew we didn't *have* to be here. We wanted to take art. We had *chosen* to be here. Teachers like that.

In fact, Rachel wanted to be some kind of visual artist when she grew up. Her stuff was hanging all over the halls. But today she seemed distracted. The grape bumps were turning out to be the edge of the blue-striped bowl.

Not her best work, but I didn't say anything.

"You know, I've been thinking," I said to Rachel when Mrs.

Fein moved on to critique the group at the next table. "Maybe *I* should have a bat mitzvah."

There, I said it even before I knew what I was saying, because in truth this was the first time the thought ever occurred to me. But once it came out, it seemed to make sense.

Rachel laughed. "Then *you'd* have to invite Lauren Chase too," she said.

I don't think she realized I was being serious.

Nana Told Me This Story Once

I remember she told me her family lived in Brooklyn, in
Brownsville. Her father owned a candy shop on Pitkin Avenue.
I already knew my grandmother was the youngest of nine children. The Gozinsky kids from Saratoga Avenue. I only knew
two of my grandmother's sisters, Bea and Rose, but they both
lived in Florida and I had met them one or two times. Back
then, when my grandmother was growing up with five brothers
and four sisters, she told me they had been very poor.

My grandmother had the usual stories about sharing a bed,
sharing clothes, shoes with worn soles. No meat for dinner.
Sometimes no dinner.

Oh, c'mon, Nana.
You want to listen or you want to ask questions?

She told me she had no toys, no games, no dolls.

And one day she was out with her mother doing errands. She must have been very young, four or five years old.

"Wait here, Freidaleh," her mother said to her. "I am going into the butcher shop. Wait right here and don't move."

Freidaleh? But your name is Freida, isn't it? Everyone calls you Freddie.

Yes, but not then. My mother added that to all our names. She called my sister Bea, Berthaleh. She called my sister Min, Mineleh.

Like shayna maideleh? *I asked.*

Exactly.

For a long time, Freida did as her mother told her. She waited on the street. She had watched her mother disappear into the shop, and she waited. She leaned against the building behind her. She looked down at the patches in her dress and the holes worn into her shoes, and that's when she noticed a big store directly across the street.

She didn't know why she hadn't seen it before. She had been to this street many, many times. Maybe because she was so little and the crowd was so thick and the people were so tall. But she saw it now. A wide glass window, and inside were shelves and shelves of toys. Freida had never had a new toy of her own.

You've told me that story before, Nana.

What story?

About how you never had any toys, no presents. No dolls.

It's no story. It's true.

Well, you've told me it before.

So now I'm telling you again. Do you want to hear the story or not?
I do.

Freida was like a little pony, stamping her feet, trying to stay still to do as her mother had told her. But as she watched, a beautiful young woman holding the hand of her young daughter entered the huge toy store. Freida couldn't stand it any longer. The little daughter looked to be about Freida's age, but that's where the similarity ended. This little girl was wearing a hat, a beautiful straw hat with a ribbon, and white gloves. Her dress was clean and had no patches. Her shoes were new. Her socks were starched white and they were about to disappear out of Freida's sight.

Freida darted out across the street and got to the window just in time to see the little girl and her beautiful mother walk inside the store, still holding hands.

Freida pressed her face against the glass and watched them. They walked up and down the aisles, the little girl smiling and pointing to everything. Then finally they seemed to have made a decision. Freida watched as the mother reached up to take down a doll from the top shelf. The doll looked almost identical to the little girl herself. The straw hat, the white dress and socks. When the mother stretched her arm up, the strap of her pocketbook slid off her shoulder. She handed the doll to her daughter, readjusted her strap, and for a while Freida couldn't see them anymore.

The street was busy with cars. People passed by in both directions. Freida turned back and looked toward the butcher shop to see if her mother had come out yet.

I should go back, she thought to herself. *My mother will be worried.*

Nora Raleigh Baskin

Just then the beautiful mother and the little girl with the hat, now holding her new doll, strolled out of the store. They turned right and began to walk in Freida's direction. For a moment, the two girls were face to face.

Eye to eye. Toe to toe.

Oh no, Nana. Did you take her doll?

Of course not.

Then what? What happened? Something must have happened.

The little girl stopped when she saw Freida. She clutched her doll even more tightly in her arms and stuck out her tongue, which proved to be more than Freida could possibly take. Right in front of the mother, and in the presence of all of Brownsville, Brooklyn, five-year-old Freida Gozinky hauled back and slapped the little girl right across the face.

No, you didn't!

I did. It left a big white handprint on her red cheek.

Omigod. What happened then?

Nothing. I ran away. I ran all the way around the block and hid on somebody's stoop. I stayed there, crying and crying, until I was sure they had gone. I felt terrible. I still feel terrible today.

Nana, it was a hundred years ago.

Well, I wouldn't say that.

So that's it? That's the story?

Yup.

Bloomie's in Winter

Practically every time we went to New York City to visit my grandmother she took me to Bloomingdale's at least once during my stay. She loved to shop and I was like the perfect excuse to do it again. Sometimes Poppy would go with us, but usually he just waited at home with Sammy. He said his circulation was bad, and his feet hurt when he walked too far on city pavement. Besides, it was his day off from work. He liked to relax and listen to Nat King Cole on his new CD player.

"I'll be here when you two beautiful ladies get back," he'd tell us. He'd winked at me. Then just as we were leaving, he'd slip me a single dollar bill and whisper that I shouldn't spend it all in one place. He was always making jokes like that.

But especially every December, even the one right before my nana got sick and I wasn't paying enough attention to notice, we went to Bloomingdale's. Any other time, the mobs of people walking down the street would just pass right by all the storefront windows of Bloomingdale's and Saks and Lord & Taylor. But in December all those stores put out ropes and barriers to hold back the lines and keep the crowds in order. People came from all over, not just to shop for the holiday but for a chance to look at the window displays. They were amazing. It was like a minitrip to Disneyland. Inside the windows were moving, singing, lit-up Christmas scenes. Mechanical figures, fake snow, moving sleds and reindeer. Every window, a different scene. Every store, a different theme.

All about Christmas.

And close by was the biggest Christmas tree in the world, at Rockefeller Center, all decorated with miles and miles of colored lights. My grandmother made sure we walked right by it on our way to Bloomingdale's.

"Are you getting too cold, my *shayna maideleh*?" my nana asked me. She was holding my hand in hers, leather glove wrapped around wool mitten. We had been standing for a while waiting for the line to move. There were even people in store uniforms that gently urged the crowd along when someone took a little too long at one window. The line wrapped around the velvet ropes three times.

"A little," I said.

I really wasn't that interested in the window displays. I knew it was my grandmother who loved them. "But I'm fine," I added. "I can wait."

"I can see them anytime," my grandmother said. "I thought you wanted to see them."

"Nah, not really, Nana."

She tugged at my arm and pulled me out of the line. "Let's go inside, then."

In and up we went, directly to the girls' department, with the toy section in the back corner. It wasn't big, not like FAO Schwarz, and it was mostly collectible toys—fancy train sets, expensive stuffed animals. And dolls.

She walked right up to the glass display counter. The Madame Alexander dolls were all on display. Some on the shelves in the counter and more on the shelves against the wall. "For your holiday present this year," my grandmother began. "Which one do you want?" That's what she always called it, a "holiday present," I think so she wouldn't hurt anybody's feelings.

My grandmother had already bought me three other Madame Alexander dolls. To start my collection.

I wish I could have told her I didn't like them. I had never played with dolls very much, even when I was little. But when I had, I liked tiny dolls, miniature things. Little people and animals you could move around with your hands, hide in your pocket, stick in the soap dish in the bathtub, bury in the dirt in the backyard after a good rain.

Madame Alexander dolls were about three feet tall and they were dressed in elaborate costumes from all over the world. And they were really expensive.

"How about the Argentina girl?" my grandmother asked me.

I shrugged. She was pretty, with her red shirt and vest, her black hair. The girl from India was beautiful too; her dress looked sheer and silky wrapped around her body from her feet to her head.

"Look at the girl from Turkey. Oh, look at those little sandals."

I shrugged again. "You don't *have* to get me a present, Nana," I said.

Nora Raleigh Baskin

"Of course I do," she said. She was trying to get closer to the shelves behind the counter. Then she stopped. She put her purse down on the glass and turned to me.

"You don't like these dolls, do you?" she asked me.

I looked down at the ground, at the gray carpet, at a little round stain. When I touched it with my shoe, it was sticky.

"Caroline. Look at me."

I did. She was smiling. "You never liked these dolls, did you?"

I shook my head.

"But you let me buy them for you."

I nodded.

"Because you knew I wanted them, didn't you?"

I nodded again.

My grandmother took me into her arms and drew me toward her. I could smell her sweet perfume right though her clothes. It would settle in my hair and on my sweater, and when I went to bed that night I would smell it on me.

"I wish I could buy one for you, Nana. For a Christmas present."

"I don't need a doll," she said. "I've got everything I could ever want, right here with me. Right now."

I was so relieved.

We made our way back to the apartment the exact way we had come. I was hoping Poppy had already ordered the Chinese food. He knew just what to get. We got the same thing every time. There were still tons of people in the streets, still a line waiting to see the window displays. I could see the red fabric and white fur trim of a mechanical Santa Claus throwing his head back as he listened to the mechanical little boy on his lap. I could hear the Christmas music piped out through speakers to the whole world. You could still hear it two blocks away.

"Oh no, Nana," I said suddenly.

"What's wrong?"

"I meant *Hanukkah*. I meant the doll could be for your Hanukkah present, right?"

It was getting dark already. We walked close together and as quickly as we could. My nana squeezed my hand tightly. "Yes, my *shayna maideleh*. For Hanukkah."

17

Plenty to Worry About

I decided to try on my Jewish star necklace again. And this time, I would wear it to school and see how it fit me.

So to speak.

Nobody would even have to see it. Not yet.

I wore it under an old long-sleeved shirt I had, one with a high collar. I thought maybe I would bring up the subject of a bat mitzvah this afternoon. Then, when I was ready, I could pull down my collar and show my mother I had been wearing my necklace, that I was sincere.

"Caroline, are you going to wear that to school?" my mother was asking me. Thursday was her day off. She was in her bathrobe. Her hair was tumbled all around her head. She had a cup of coffee in her hand.

Sammy had taken his breakfast into the den to watch ESPN and my dad had wandered by and gotten stuck there watching highlights of a baseball game I knew for certain they had watched just last night.

My mother and I were alone in the kitchen. Had she seen my necklace with her X-ray vision? Did she know?

I looked down at myself as best I could. "Wear what?"

"That shirt," she said.

I was so relieved, I got confused. If she hadn't seen my necklace, why was she concerned about my shirt? Of all the things my mother did to annoy me, she never hassled me about my clothes.

"What's wrong with this shirt?" I asked.

She lowered her voice. "I just thought you might want to wear an undershirt or even one of those bras I bought you, Caroline. That shirt is a little clingy."

Oh, God. That's what she was talking about?

My skin, my face, flushed with a sudden heat of embarrassment as if just that moment I became aware of myself. I materialized in solid form, whereas a minute ago I was invisible. A minute ago I was just a kid. And for no reason at all, tears sprang into my eyes.

"Oh, sweetie. I'm sorry," my mother said. "Here, come on. Let's go into your room. I can drive you to school a little late. Come on."

After Sam and my dad left, I let my mom show me what she was talking about, even though I already knew. I had seen it in other girls, little lumps of flesh that practically screamed nakedness. My mother took out the two little bras she had bought me and put in my drawer about a month ago. One was tan, one was white.

I was just about to take off my shirt with my mom in my room when I remembered I was wearing my Jewish star.

"No, Mom. Don't look. Don't! Turn around," I shouted. I

had my arms crossed, my hands holding either side of my shirt—the shirt that, now that I knew it was practically see-through, I would never wear again as long as I lived.

She laughed. "Okay. Okay." She turned her back to me and made my bed as I got undressed. "But, sweetie, we've all got them."

But we don't all have this, I thought.

We don't all have a religious symbol hanging around our neck. For a second I caught a glimpse of myself in my mirror, my bony collarbone, my bare shoulders, and the glint of gold resting just at my neck. What would Mom think? Would it make her happy or sad? Would she think I was trying to be someone I wasn't? Would she roll her eyes at me like I was just a child? Like I was hypocritical? Two-faced? Just plain silly?

I didn't feel like finding out. Not now.

I quickly undid the clasp and slipped the necklace back into the top drawer of my dresser. I pulled the elastic bra, the tan-colored one, down over my head, slipped my arms in, and adjusted it over my chest.

"Okay, now you can look," I said, turning around.

"You're a woman now," my mother said. "Just imagine that."

"I can't," I answered. "I'm not ready."

"Nobody feels *really* ready. Ever. If you waited until you felt totally ready for something, you'd probably be waiting forever. You'd never try anything new."

I wanted to tell her my idea. Right now. It was perfect.

"How do you think I got through medical school?" She laughed.

Mom, I want to be Jewish too. Like you. I want to know funny little Yiddish words. Like Nana and Poppy. I want to know what you do on Yom Kippur. Like Rachel.

I need a bat mitzvah.

But my mother was already standing up. "Oh, by the way," she said. "Poppy is coming up here with Aunt Gert. They want to visit before Gert leaves for the winter in Florida."

"When?"

"This weekend. Why?"

"But this weekend is that sleepover. At Lauren's!"

"Who?"

"Lauren Chase, Mom. Saturday. Mom, I told you. You said I could go."

"Not to worry." My mother kissed the top of my head. "Sunday. They're coming Sunday."

My I-think-I-maybe-want-a-bat-mitzvah speech and the necklace would have to wait for another day. Suddenly, I was reminded of more important things to worry about.

18

What I Need

Rachel's invitation came in the mail that very Saturday. I had known that she and her mother made them by hand, but when I opened it, I couldn't even tell. Except that it was so special. It was gold paper. No, I couldn't say gold, exactly, more like copper, with a border of purple along one side. In the center, also bordered in purple, was a white paper announcement:

Please join us in celebration of our daughter
רחל יעל
RACHEL YAEL
BECOMING A BAT MITZVAH
SATURDAY, DECEMBER EIGHTH
TWO THOUSAND AND SEVEN
AT TEN-FIFTEEN IN THE MORNING
TEMPLE SHALOM
259 RICHARDS AVENUE
KIDDUSH LUNCHEON FOLLOWING SERVICES
SANDI AND JAY MILLER

At the very top, on the copper paper, were three perfectly placed lavender-colored gems and more Hebrew letters, with the translation:

Make for me a holy place so that I may dwell among you.

There was a phone number and even an e-mail address just for RSVPs. RachelsBmitzvah@aol.com.

I held the invitation in my hand, turning it over and feeling the weight of it. It had been addressed to my whole family, Sammy too, because, as Rachel had told me, we were family friends. Not just friend-friends. I ran my finger over the three little stones glued to the top of the page. They held fast.

I thought about all the people who were getting this invitation today. Rachel had invited her entire family, cousins and relatives she didn't even know but who wanted to come and share this event with her. People were going to make plane reservations now and book hotel rooms.

"You ready to go?"

I nearly dropped the invitation on the kitchen floor.

"Dad?" I turned around.

"To your party, Car. Isn't it time? Don't we have to pick Rachel up?"

I had that kind of look, like I was doing something wrong. I dropped Rachel's invitation on the counter, like I had just broken something or I was sneaking extra cookies, even though, of course, I wasn't. But when my dad looked at me, I could tell he thought the same thing.

"I'll be ready in a minute, Dad. Don't forget Sammy's sleeping bag for Rachel," I called out behind me. I was already halfway up the stairs.

I threw my clothes into an overnight bag. Pajamas, two pairs, depending on what the other girls wore. Clothes for tomorrow: clean jeans, a shirt, another sweater, new socks, two pairs of underpants, and my one extra bra. You never know.

I threw in my toothbrush, hairbrush, and my iPod in case I couldn't sleep, which happens to me sometimes. And then just before I headed out the door I opened my grandmother's bottle of perfume. I put my nose right up to the top.

If there were a genie in that bottle, she would have appeared right before my eyes. And she would have looked just like my nana. Actually, it wasn't like I could *see* her, but suddenly I could feel her. I wanted to know what she would tell me if she were here.

I knew what I would ask.

"Don't come up," I shouted down to my dad as I passed the landing of the stairs on my way to my parents' bedroom. "I'll be right there."

I went into my parents' bathroom.

There, I thought so.

My mother had cotton balls in her medicine cabinet.

I turned the tiny bottle upside down against the cotton very quickly, up and down. I didn't want to waste it. This was all I had. I could see a tiny spot of golden soaking into the fluffy cotton. I carefully put the top on and the bottle back in my room, and then right before I flew down the stairs and out to the car, I tucked the cotton ball under the elastic of my bra. The tan one.

If she could hear me, I knew what I would say.

Maybe I could have a bat mitzvah, Nana.

And then I'd be Jewish too.

You Don't Look Jewish

Lauren's house was massive. My dad didn't seem to notice, but if he had, he wouldn't have cared. My mother and father are not impressed with things like that. He dropped off Rachel and me and all our stuff at the front door. He introduced himself to Mrs. Chase—"Pick-up time is noon tomorrow"—and then he was off.

We walked inside, into a cavernous hall, and I missed him already.

I used to get homesick at sleepovers all the time, even at Rachel's, long past the age it was more acceptable. So even in fifth grade my dad would sometimes have to come and pick me up in the middle of the night. I remember once, I had fallen asleep waiting for him to show up, after I broke down crying and wanting to go home. I heard him come into the dark house. My friend—whoever it was, I don't remember—was already fast asleep. I heard the mom talking to my dad, laughing softly, telling him not to worry. No problem, she was saying. And I pretended to stay asleep. I kept my eyes shut as he carried me out to the warm car and slipped me into the backseat.

I felt so safe and comfortable listening to the vibrations of the car and my dad's soft humming as we rode toward home. Later I would act as if I had been disappointed in myself for being such a baby, but secretly I loved it. I loved knowing I could go home anytime I wanted.

All I had to do was call and it would be there waiting for me.

And wouldn't you know it, we were the first girls to get to Lauren's.

"I hope you remembered, no gifts," Lauren sang to us as she led us up the stairs.

"Right," Rachel said. She was right behind Lauren, pulling herself up along the white banister.

"Maybe I should leave a trail of bread crumbs in case we have to find our way out," I said. I was the last in line.

"What?" Lauren asked.

"It was a joke," I said out loud. "Forget it. It was silly. Your house is so big." Rachel and I were dragging our sleeping bags and overnight stuff. About an hour later we made it into Lauren's bedroom.

"Wow," I said. Rachel just nodded.

First of all, it was big, really big. So big there were two sections to it. A sleep/play side and more of a work/study side, as best I could tell. Lauren's computer and everything that went along with that—speakers and wires, printer, and DVD player— sat on a lacquered desk module-type thing, with shelves and drawers and a leather chair on wheels pushed underneath. The floor was carpeted but there were also rugs on top of it, one that matched her bedspread (pink) and another that matched the color of her computer desk (red).

"Y'all can spread your beds here," Lauren instructed us. "Mother will get some air mattresses later."

"Then when everyone else gets here"—Lauren was talking really fast—"we are going to bake cookies, do each other's hair and nails. And before the movie and popcorn we can steam our faces and use the all-natural clay and seaweed facial Mother bought for us. Oh, someone's here!"

When the doorbell rang downstairs, Lauren bounded out, leaving Rachel and me standing in the center of the room, still holding our bags.

"Why are we here?" I asked Rachel.

She shook her head slowly.

"Do you know who else is coming?"

She shook her head again. She couldn't speak. In a funny way, even though Rachel was more sure of herself than I was, she was more afraid of things. Right now she looked like she was in shock—medical shock, like I should lay her down, cover her with a blanket, and rub her extremities to improve circulation.

"It will be fun, Rach."

But it wasn't.

It was horrible.

Only it wasn't because of the manicures or the facials. Or the movie or hair-braiding session that lasted two hours. It wasn't even because Rachel and I were apparently the only ones who thought Lauren had been sincere in telling people not to bring gifts.

Mandy Richards bought Lauren the latest Harry Potter book.

Jamie Lewine gave her a pair of chandelier earrings.

Stephanie Curtis's gift was personalized stationery and a matching pen.

Zoe Kupper was thoughtful enough to give Lauren a packet of movie passes to the local theater.

"You *didn't* think she was serious," Mandy whispered to me while Lauren was trying on her new earrings. "Nobody means it when they say that. Don't you know that?"

Even that wasn't even the worst part.

The worst part happened after the lights went out, when we were all spread out on our air mattresses (there were enough for all six of us), with Lauren sitting up on her bed with a flashlight, which she had just turned off. My cell phone said it was just after one o'clock in the morning.

I was really tired. My eyelids burned. My legs ached. I wanted to fall asleep so it would be morning. Because if it were morning, my dad would be here soon. Or Rachel's mom. Or Rachel's dad. I forgot who was picking up us at noon, only ten hours and fifty-two minutes from now.

Whoopee.

It was completely dark in the room. Lauren was still doing most of the talking. In fact, I could probably fall asleep if she *weren't* talking. Or if I wasn't so worried about somebody stepping on me. Or drawing on my face with a marker while I was sleeping. It seemed like that kind of crowd to me.

Up until then, actually, it hadn't been so bad. Rachel and I had fun painting our nails and taking sticky film pictures of ourselves in green face masks. Lauren's mother was pretty nice. She brought us food and kept telling us to make ourselves at home. Lauren had an older sister, but we never saw her.

I turned over, trying to get comfortable. I wasn't worried

anymore about being homesick. I was too tired.

"Oh, by the way, Rachel?" Lauren's voice was faceless in the dark, but it was definitely hers. "Rachel?"

"I'm awake," Rachel responded, but I think she had already fallen asleep, if only just a second ago. She was right next to me, her head on her pillow. Her eyes were closed. "What?"

"I got your invitation today," Lauren said.

"Oh."

I knew that no one else at this party had been invited to Rachel's bat mitzvah. It would be rude to talk about it here. So either Lauren was really thoughtless or really nasty. I wasn't sure. Her Virginia accent made it hard to tell.

"It was really pretty."

"Thanks," Rachel said, making her voice as small as she could.

"It's my first bat mitzvah invitation," Lauren told us all.

Clearly Rachel didn't want to talk about it here, and it could have been all over right then.

"But I didn't know you were *Jewish*," Lauren went on. "Well, you know, Miller isn't a Jewish name or anything."

Rachel didn't respond.

I knew Rachel better than anyone in that room, and I knew in one more second, if Lauren didn't shut up, Rachel was going to start crying.

"So *what*?" I answered, in a voice a little louder and a little stronger than Rachel's had been, the way you would distract a predator away from its victim. And encourage it to attack you instead.

Lauren turned right toward me. "I just didn't know it, that's all," she said. "Rachel doesn't even look Jewish."

Yarmulkes, *Peyes*, and the Asian Rain Forest

When we were in fourth grade, our entire class took a trip to the Bronx Zoo. We took coach buses, and after an hour on Interstate 95, we got stuck in a long line of traffic just outside the park, mostly other school buses. We were later than we were supposed to be, but we got there. Everyone poured off the bus. We didn't get to pick our groups and sometimes I think the teachers purposely put us with kids who aren't our friends. Which is to say, I wasn't with Rachel and Rachel wasn't with me. I was in a group with Anna McGee and Owen and Gareth Rees, twin boys in my grade. Mrs. Rees was our chaperone, but she didn't seem cut out for either chaperoning or mothering two twin boys who couldn't stand still. She was, in my mother's words, a nervous wreck.

The zoo was mobbed, as if every school in the tri-state area had chosen the same day for their school trip.

"Stay with me. Owen. Gareth. Everyone. Girls, please,"

Mrs. Rees kept saying. Anna and I were right beside her the whole time. Her two sons were trying to step on each other's shoes and it slowed them down a bit.

"Not to worry. The boys are right behind us," I said.

There were so many people around us, so much noise, I had to shout. We had a map and a list of required sights to see given to us by the school, but we could visit them in any order. I had the map. Anna had the list. We all wore tags around our necks with the name of our school—as did, it seemed, every kid in the whole zoo, all in different colors and logos.

"They're just goofing around, Mrs. Rees. We can go," Anna said.

Mrs. Rees was flustered but she started ahead with a bolt. "Okay, we'll do the Asian rain forest first," she said. "This way."

We were all about to cross the pedestrian walk and head up the path to the Asian rain forest when we suddenly had to stop. Only Mrs. Rees had made it across—the rest of us had to wait as a large group of boys and their teacher crossed in front of us. None of them had tags around their necks, but you could tell they were all together because they all looked exactly the same. Well, almost. They were dressed identically, in black suits and white shirts even though it was hot out, little black yarmulkes on their heads, and they each had two long curls of hair bouncing at the sides of their heads.

I knew they were Jewish children. Sometimes in Manhattan I would see a man dressed just like that. My grandmother once explained it to me when I asked her about him.

He's Orthodox, she told me then. Orthodox are very religious Jews, very observant of all the traditions. Even the way they dress. Even the way the boys wear their hair, the long side curls called *peyes*.

Nora Raleigh Baskin

"What's up with them?" Owen said out loud after the last in the group of boys had passed. We all began to walk again.

"They're Jewish," Anna explained.

Mrs. Rees was waiting for us on the other side, trying to suppress her frantic look at having been divided from her charges. She was waving at us to hurry up.

"Well, I know lots of Jewish people who don't look like that," Owen said. The two boys started ahead, Anna and I beside them on either side.

"Yeah, I don't get it," Gareth said. "Why would anyone want to look so weird like that if they didn't have to?"

I knew what Gareth was saying wasn't nice, and that if a grown-up had been around, he probably wouldn't have said it at all. Then I wondered what Rachel would have done if she were here. Would she have said something? Just because they were Jewish and so was she? At the same time, I remember thinking Owen was right. They *did* look weird, certainly different and pretty strange. Rachel was Jewish and she didn't look like that. I didn't get it.

"Yeah, really," I said out loud. "They look so weird." And just then, I turned to see that one of the little boys had fallen behind his group.

He was dressed all in black, long pants and a jacket, with a white shirt. He had clear blue eyes, a short haircut with two long wisps of blond in front of his ears, a black yarmulke right there, on top of his head. And he was stopped in the middle of the road, looking right at me. Listening.

Hey, It's a Compliment

"She doesn't look Jewish? What's that supposed to mean, Lauren?" I blurted out.

"You know . . . ," Lauren said. "Everyone knows what I mean. It's not a big deal."

"Yes, it is," I heard myself saying.

One of the girls drew in her breath. But I didn't care. I could sense everyone tensing. Hoping to avoid something unpleasant. Hoping it would all go away.

But this was unpleasant and it wasn't going to go away.

"Well . . . ," Lauren lilted. "Rachel has blond hair for one thing."

"So what?" I snapped back.

I'm Jewish, I could say. *And I find what you are saying very insulting.*

But then again, I wasn't really Jewish, was I? I didn't know anything about it. *You're not even having a bat mitzvah.* Lauren could say that, couldn't she? She could say all that. And she'd be right.

"So she's blond," Lauren went on. "And her nose, you know . . ."

"What about it?" I asked. I had no idea what she meant or what Lauren was going to say.

"Her nose is so small," Lauren said. "It's a compliment, for Pete's sake, Caroline. Lighten up."

I felt my hand rise up and touch my nose. My hair was not blond. It was dark and curly. Was this what I wanted? If not looking Jewish was a compliment, then what was Lauren saying? It didn't feel good. It was scary.

I opened my eyes as wide as I could, letting every available bit of light inside. I could now make out Lauren, now lying down on her pillow. Her arms folded over her chest. What is darkness, after all? A measure of what is missing.

Maybe all you had to do was look more closely, open wide your eyes.

Rachel still wasn't saying anything.

"A compliment?" My voice was loud. I knew Lauren's mother might walk in. Or her father. Someone might come and tell us all to settle down, but it would be me they would be talking to. I was the one sitting up.

With my fists tight. My big mouth open.

Lauren must have had the same worry. She had her other guests to consider. Her mother. Her party's reputation.

"Listen, Caroline, it's none of your business," Lauren said.

"It's sure not *your* business," I shot back.

"Look, I *liked* the invitation, Caroline," Lauren went on. "I just said I didn't know she was Jewish. Big deal. Anyway, I didn't want to invite you to my sleepover in the first place. Your friend Rachel made me. So there."

I was stunned.

Defeated on two fronts, and it was all over.

Nobody talked any more the rest of the night. The hours and minutes glowed one after another every time I pressed the display on my cell phone. But eventually, I fell asleep. When I woke up, the first thing I felt was that little ball of cotton. It must have stayed pressed to my skin when I took off my clothes and got into pajamas the night before. I had forgotten about it and now it was stuck to my cheek.

I pulled it off. It was flat and flecked with little bits of lint from the inside of my sleeping bag, but it was still strongly scented. I held it to my nose.

And wanted to cry.

But I waited.

Rachel and I hadn't talked much in the morning. Lauren acted as if nothing had happened. We had blueberry pancakes with natural maple syrup from some farm stand in Vermont, which personally I hate. I like the stuff in the plastic bottle with the picture of the woman with the kerchief on her head, smiling at me.

When I got home, I ran upstairs to my room, shut the door, and landed on my bed. And then I cried.

Nora Raleigh Baskin

Just When I Thought I Couldn't Take One More Thing

My head was spinning. I didn't know what I was more upset about, getting into a fight, trying to be something I didn't even know I wanted to be, or how embarrassed I felt when Lauren said what she said.

No, I knew.

I was more upset that everyone heard I hadn't really been invited to Lauren's party. So I had been right. Lauren never wanted to invite me.

I was a loser, and now I was a loser and a phony. A poser. And a horrible friend because I embarrassed myself and Rachel. What would I say to Rachel, after I had ruined our chances of ever getting invited to an A-list party again? After I had made such a fool out of myself.

I felt like I did in my dream, thrashing around in the ocean, afraid and alone. Not having anything to hold on to.

"Caroline, are you all right?" My mother came into my room.

I knew she had come up to tell me that my grandfather and his sister were here. And she knew I was upset as soon as she saw my face. I thought about telling her everything. About the sleepover invitation that never was. About what a poor job I did trying to stick up for Rachel. What a poor job I did trying to stick up for myself. Maybe I could tell her about what Lauren said, because I knew that would make my mom really furious. She might not be so Jewish, but she was big on causes and all things unjust.

But this time she got it all wrong.

"I know you're not crazy about seeing your aunt Gert today," she said.

"What?" I wiped my eyes.

"Caroline, I know you overheard what Daddy and I were talking about in the car. I've been meaning to talk to you about that."

"What?" I said it again.

"I know you heard me saying things about Poppy and his family and why they haven't been in touch all these years. I shouldn't have been talking about it in the car like that. I was just very upset, after the funeral and everything."

"Mom . . ."

"But it was a long time ago, Caroline. It's good they have each other again . . . if Poppy can forgive his sister, certainly we can. So do you think you can come downstairs and be nice. For me?" she said.

I didn't move from my bed but at least I wasn't crying anymore. Maybe it would be a good time to talk to her. She was in one of her talking moods. Of course, it would have been better if she had been in a listening mood. I opened my mouth but didn't know where to start. I never got to.

"I mean, Caroline," my mother went on suddenly, "it's not like *my* parents were so thrilled when I wanted to marry your father."

I had no idea what she was talking about. Nana and Poppy? "Huh?"

"Because Daddy wasn't Jewish," she explained. "Poppy even offered to buy me a new car if I didn't get married." She laughed.

That wasn't funny at all, I thought.

"So come on downstairs, sweetie. Okay? Daddy's making his specialty tuna fish salad."

"Aunt Gert is here already?" I asked.

She nodded.

"Okay, I'll be right there," I said.

I mean, really, I didn't think my life could get any worse.

I fell into bed exhausted that night, but it was still hard to fall asleep. I kept thinking about the whole weekend, about everything that had happened. It was like a whole lifetime had gone by. It was like I had been a little kid Friday and I was an old lady by Sunday night.

I knew too much, I thought. And nothing at all.

I couldn't sleep.

I thought about that little orthodox boy. What was he doing now? Would he tell people the story of what happened to him at the Bronx Zoo one day, about the girl who called him weird? Or did that happen to him all the time? Had I hurt his feelings?

I hadn't meant anything by it, but probably neither had Lauren.

And I kept thinking about my nana and Poppy and about what would have happened if my mother had decided she really wanted a new car after all. I might not be here right now.

At least then I'd have nothing to worry about.

And just before I finally settled down and was about to fall asleep, I remembered tomorrow was picture day.

Great.

I Will Be Like Me

You know how just before you are going to get your hair cut, it looks really good? Your mother calls this fancy place weeks before because you're complaining so much, then the very day of your appointment, your hair looks great. It looks the best it ever has and you wonder why you ever wanted to get it cut in the first place.

Well, that's *not* what my day was like.

Monday morning, picture day, my hair decided to have a life of its own.

I probably should have washed it the night before, but I had thought it would be too frizzy. Now I looked like a squirrel. There was one big knot in the back I couldn't get out. I tugged at it.

"Mom!" I called out. "I need help."

I could hear the water running. I could hear my dad and Sammy talking downstairs, so that meant it was my mom in the shower. I looked at my clock. The bus came in fifteen minutes. I was on my own. I couldn't remember what background we had picked for the photos, so I didn't know what color shirt to wear. Last year I wore a purple shirt against the green background and it looked like puke.

I needed something neutral. Black or white or gray. I didn't own anything gray. My favorite white long-sleeved T-shirt was in the wash. It could be there for weeks. I had a black cotton turtleneck, and if I stretched the neck out so it hung loose, it looked pretty good on me. It was a little early, still warm outside—the beginning of October—but I thought I could get away with it.

I finally got my hair combed neatly. It hung pretty straight, shiny and dark. I had a little clear mascara that I combed across my eyebrows to keep them in line. I pinched my cheeks to make them red. I rolled my strawberry lip gloss over my lips. I looked into my bedroom mirror. What did I want people to see? I practiced a smile or two that I could use for my individual picture.

A face that I sort of knew, but sort of didn't, smiled back.

That's when I took out the necklace from the top drawer of my dresser for the third time. I didn't hesitate. I unhooked the clasp and reached my arms around the back of my neck. I couldn't see the mechanism but I could feel it, and with my fingers I fit the two pieces back together. It locked into place and hung perfectly around my neck.

You could barely see the delicate links of the chain under the fold of the turtleneck, but the pendant was like a golden star in a black sky. Today I would wear my necklace.

Things Are Looking Up Already

"I like your necklace," Megan said to me when I got on the bus and sat down on the seat next to her. I shoved my backpack under my feet and rested my hands on my knees.

"Oh, thanks," I said.

She didn't say anything, but I was so ready with my answer that I gave it to her anyway.

"I'm Jewish," I told her. "I mean I'm half and half. Sort of."

"Really?"

"Well, my mom is Jewish and my dad isn't."

"Oh."

I got the feeling Megan wasn't all that interested, but I went on. "I just found out that my grandparents didn't want my mom to marry my dad because he wasn't Jewish. They tried to bribe her with a car. So I'm not sure what I am, really."

"What do you mean?"

"I mean . . ."

We were coming up to Ryan Berk's stop.

"I mean, if I'm Jewish it might upset my dad, right? And my mom doesn't care either way. In fact, I get the feeling that if I wanted to be Jewish, it would upset her, too. Because of that car thing, you know?"

"Boy, that's funny," Megan said.

The bus hissed as it slowed down.

"It is, isn't it?"

The doors opened and Ryan appeared on the steps and then inside the bus. He never looked at me once. He walked right by and headed all the way to the back.

"He likes you," Megan said.

"What?"

"Ryan Berk. He likes you, you can tell. By the way he never looks at you."

"He does? No, he doesn't," I said. Did he? And as ridiculous as Megan's theory sounded, I found myself wanting it to be true. "How do you know?"

"He goes out of his way not to look at you," Megan went on. "I've been noticing for weeks now."

"Really?"

The bus stopped at school and as always everyone stood up instantly. We used to have a bus driver named Mr. Mackey who made us exit the bus one row at a time, starting in the back, in perfect order. You weren't even allowed to stand until the seat behind you had emptied.

But that was then. Mr. Mackey retired last year.

Now it was every man for himself. The biggest and strongest, or fastest and smallest, got into the aisle first and headed for the bus doors.

Nora Raleigh Baskin

Unless, of course, someone stopped for you. And *if* someone halted right at your seat and waited for you to get out, holding up everyone behind them, well, that was big. It definitely meant something.

"Caroline?"

I looked up. Ryan Berk was standing by my seat, holding up the line and every single kid behind him, now shoving forward eagerly to get off the bus. He had stopped to let *me* out.

I was in the outside seat, Megan by the window. She nudged me.

"You can go now," she whispered, in case I hadn't noticed Ryan waiting.

But of course, I had. How could I have missed that?

My Star of David

We were all in one long line in the sixth-grade hallway. I was feeling pretty good so far. Walking into school with Ryan Berk was definitely a good way to start the morning. I could barely keep the smile off my face, which might not be a bad thing for picture day.

Each class had a specific time to report to the library, where the photographer was all set up. The photographers always run late. They always get the little plaque with the teacher's name wrong, and somebody always slips off the little bleachers or makes rabbit ears or generally screws things up for the first shot.

"I'm going to steal a bunch of those free combs," Brandon Newkirk said to no one in particular.

"Isn't that an oxymoron, you moron?" Nikki Cooper whispered to Brandon Newkirk. I was right behind Nikki Cooper, and Sebastian Charles was right behind me.

If we went in alphabetical order by teacher names there was

a good chance Rachel's homeroom class would be right after mine and I'd see her as we left the library. But I wished she were here now.

I wanted to ask her again if she thought I should have a bat mitzvah. I wanted to show her my necklace, that I was wearing it. I was dying to tell her about Ryan Berk.

After about three more minutes, kids started pushing. Sebastian Charles bumped into me, me into Nikki, and Nikki into Brandon.

"Get control of yourself, Nikki. I mean, I knew you liked me, but this is ridiculous," Brandon said.

"Oh, shut up," Nikki told him.

Three minutes more and two boys were physically fighting down at the end of the line.

"Okay, I've had it. We're going in," our homeroom teacher announced. She opened the library door. "Everyone just take a seat."

It looked like the class before us was just finishing. They were coming down off their places on the bleachers. The photographer looked completely exasperated already. It was only eight thirty in the morning. There was a certain amount of confusion as our two classes filled the room, avoiding the bleachers, the camera stand, and the backdrops. Teachers hate these moments.

It was pretty much a free-for-all.

I looked over to see Brandon reaching into the box with the combs. And that's when I saw Lauren Chase. I didn't know she was in this homeroom. But that was dumb. Why would I know who was in this homeroom? Or which homeroom Lauren Chase would be in? She was turning and heading right this way.

My mind flashed to the night of her sleepover, the darkness, and the sound of her voice.

My Star of David.

I reached up to try and tuck it into my shirt, just for a second, just for the moment we would pass each other. I don't know why. I just didn't feel like having her say anything to me. I didn't feel like answering to her, or even having her look at me. I didn't want to be different or stand out. I didn't want her to know who I was. And maybe have a reason not to like me even more than she already did.

It was none of her business.

I just needed to get my necklace off my turtleneck. If I could just pull the fabric out from under the chain and let the necklace fall inside. I had to be fast.

Quickly, before she would get here.

The chain was tight but the turtleneck should just slip out. Had she seen me? Finally, I took one good yank. I felt something snap.

"Oh, hello, Caroline." Lauren said. She barely looked at me as she made her way past and out the door.

I slapped my hand flat against my chest.

No! It couldn't be.

My necklace was gone.

I stretched my turtleneck out all the way. I reached under my shirt and felt inside my bra. I didn't even care what I looked like doing this.

No necklace. It was gone. It must have fallen completely off. Onto the floor.

There were feet everywhere. Bodies and voices. The two homeroom teachers were arguing. A whole other homeroom class had decided to come in as well. We were half an hour behind. It looked like the photographer was yelling at his assistant. Brandon Newkirk was the only one in the whole room who looked content.

I was on my hands and knees.

This couldn't be. How could I have been so stupid? So thoughtless. The chain was so fragile. It was gold. It had broken so quickly. I had only had the necklace for a couple of months. This was why my mother never let me have anything valuable.

I could feel the tears filling my eyes. They didn't run down my face, they dropped right onto the carpet.

"Caroline, what's wrong?"

It was Rachel. Her homeroom *was* next for picture taking, thank God.

"My necklace," I cried to her. "I broke it. It was my grandmother's. Her Jewish star. It's real. It snapped right off my neck."

"We'll find it," Rachel said. She was on the floor right beside me. "It's got to be here somewhere, right?"

First I tried to hide my necklace, then I broke it. I hadn't even made it five minutes without doing another stupid thing. I estimated I might begin to like myself again when I was around the age of eighty, but I was so grateful that I wouldn't be alone.

It Can't Be Broken

Rachel was explaining to me that the chain could be fixed. It was just one of the little links that was pulled apart. We had found my necklace on the floor under one of the library tables.

"It's not broken. The links can be reconnected. Right here." She showed me. "It will be fine."

"Thanks, Rachel."

"Anytime."

I held the necklace in my palm, just as I had when my grandfather first gave it to me. So much had happened since then. This necklace had come to mean so much, more than just something my grandmother wanted me to have. It had also caused so much trouble and made me think about things I never would have. But then again, maybe that's exactly what she would have wanted.

Rachel and I were sitting outside. We'd both decided to skip next period Spanish. If we got caught we'd be breaking two rules, being outside of the building without permission and cutting class. Detention for sure.

But nobody knew about this spot but us. We had discovered it one day in fourth grade when we both arrived late for school. We were trying to sneak in without passing the front office. Our spot was to the side of the cafeteria, near the big Dumpsters that blocked anyone from seeing you from the parking lot. The sun cut across the roof of the school and lay a perfectly rectangular beam of light directly onto the stoop where we sat.

Rachel called it Our Sanctuary.

"Were you mad at me?" Rachel said after we sat quietly for a few minutes.

"Me? Mad at you?"

"For asking Lauren to invite you to her party too."

"Oh, that." It did hurt when Rachel mentioned it again, sort of like a little kick in the stomach I had been able to ignore until just then.

"No," I said slowly. "What happened? Why didn't you tell me?"

"I dunno. I didn't want to hurt your feelings. But I kind of wanted to go and I thought you'd want to too."

"So what really happened?"

"Well, Lauren asked me to go," Rachel went on. "Then she asked me if I knew anybody cool. . . . I mean, it wasn't like I forced her to invite you. When I mentioned you, she said yeah, good idea."

"Would you have gone if she said she wouldn't invite me?"

"No way," Rachel answered, and I believed her with all my heart.

We were quiet. We only had another few minutes before the first bell was going to ring. You could see winter ahead—not that it was cold out yet, but you knew it was coming. The way the trees seemed prepared, the leaves turning from red to gold and some already curling brown. The ground was harder; the light from the sun was lower and not as strong.

"I wanted to thank you for what you did," Rachel said. "What you said to Lauren that night."

"What? That? I thought *you'd* be mad at *me* for ruining our chances of ever getting invited to a popular party ever again."

"Why? You were sticking up for me. For both of us, right?"

So Rachel thought I was Jewish?

That's when I understood. If that's what I wanted, I didn't have to convince anyone. The only person doubting it was me.

"Yeah, sure, for both of us—until I saw Lauren this morning and I practically tore my whole shirt off so she wouldn't see my necklace."

"Well, that's understandable. Lauren's pretty scary."

"And dumb. I think mostly she's just dumb."

"Who cares about her dumb party," Rachel said.

"Who wants to be like her, anyway?"

"Not me."

"Me neither."

Rachel laughed as the bell sounded inside the school. We both stood up and brushed the dirt from our pants. Even if I didn't get to have a bat mitzvah, that didn't mean I wasn't Jewish. I didn't need to prove anything to anyone, not to anyone but myself. I could be whatever I wanted, even Jewish.

It was mine if I wanted, like a gift that someone gave me a long time ago that I forgot to open.

Nora Raleigh Baskin

27

I Should Have Known Then

The last time Sammy and I came into the city by ourselves to visit our grandparents was probably six months ago. Nana was already sick, but I didn't know it. I guess I didn't want to.

That was the day we went to Gold's Deli. That was the day I had my first chocolate egg cream, and that was the last real day I got to spend with my nana alone.

At Gold's Deli they put a metal bowl of pickles on the table before you even order your food.

"Are they free?" Sammy asked, but he was already touching one.

"Can we just eat them?" I asked.

"It's required, in fact." My grandfather took one of the ones that was a lighter shade of green and bit it nearly in half. "My favorite," he told us. "The sour ones."

I had never seen so much activity in one restaurant. There was a counter with people lined up to get take-out sandwiches, salads, bagels. And there were small tables with checkered tablecloths and waiters, all men, older men, running all over the place. They seemed to know who had come in, who was leaving, who had ordered what, without writing anything down. They were also gruff and impatient.

"Whadda want to drink, young lady?"

I thought he was talking to me, but when I looked up from my menu he was addressing my grandmother. She smiled.

"An egg cream," she told him. "Vanilla, please. Would you like one, Caroline?"

"What is it?"

"It's good, kid. Want one? Chocolate?" the waiter said to me.

This was no time for procrastination. "Yes, please," I said. "Chocolate."

My grandmother just nibbled at her sandwich. She didn't even ask for a doggie bag. When we left we walked slowly, and at the corner we split up. My grandfather headed back to the apartment with Sammy, and Nana and I headed toward her doctor's office. We were going to get a taxicab for the ride.

"We're taking a cab?" I asked. I was excited. I liked getting into cabs. I liked the broad leather seat that sometimes didn't even have seat belts.

"I thought you liked to walk when Poppy wasn't with us?" I said. I had scooted over and I was already playing with the air-conditioner controls.

"Not today, my *shayna*," my nana said.

I noticed sometimes I was *shayna*. Sometimes *shayna madel*. And sometimes *shayna maideleh*. But I should have been paying more attention to my nana. She barely ate her lunch.

We took a cab because she was too tired to walk, and I didn't even notice it.

Nora Raleigh Baskin

28

Feels Like Snow

The Saturday afternoon my family and I were going into the city to shop for Rachel's bat mitzvah, it finally got winter cold. All along the hour-or-so drive I watched the sky get grayer and grayer and waited to see the tips of the buildings rise into view. It almost looked like snow, even though it was only the beginning of November.

"Well, I remember once it snowed on Thanksgiving," my mother said, looking out the window at the Hudson River on our right.

"Oh, sure," my dad added. "And remember when it snowed in May?" He kept his eyes forward, on the road. I had to sit in back next to Sam, who had fallen asleep almost immediately after we got in the car. Now he was snoring.

Why do grown-ups like talking about the weather?

"I don't feel so good, Mom," Sammy was saying. He had woken up, and I had to admit, he didn't look so good.

"We're almost there, sweetheart," my mother said. "You're

probably just carsick. Do you want Daddy to pull over?"

"Amy, don't tell him that. I can't just pull over on the West Side Highway," my dad said. His voice had that high-pitched, annoyed tone.

"He'll be fine," my mom told us all, including Sam.

I wasn't so sure.

It took us thirty minutes to find parking, which ended up being in an expensive hourly rate garage when we couldn't find a spot. My parents were another minute from full-fledged bickering, but once we got out of the car, things felt better. Except that Sammy was still complaining. To get even more attention, he was walking kind of bent over and holding his stomach.

We were going to take a subway downtown and then work our way back up to the department stores. First my dad wanted to go to the Barneys warehouse on West 17th Street.

"So you're Mr. Fancypants all of a sudden?" my mother joked. "Barneys?" She made herself talk with a funny accent. They both laughed and walked toward the subway stop holding hands, but we never made it that far.

"I'm really sick, Mommy," Sammy said. He had stopped in the middle of the sidewalk and had his head down.

I think it was the "Mommy" that did it.

My dad had to pick Sam up in his arms, while my mother put her hand on Sammy's forehead. She looked into his eyes while we all turned around and headed back toward the garage. And at some point during that parent powwow I heard the word "hospital."

Now my mother was in the backseat with Sammy. Asking him questions like Where does it hurt? and Does it hurt when I press here? Or here?

"New York Hospital," my mother directed. "On the East Side."

"I know where it is," my dad snapped.

I was getting scared. We got stuck in traffic and then we got lost. And then we found it. And then my mom and Sammy and I were in the emergency room and my dad was parking the car all over again.

"Is Sammy going to be all right?" I asked my mom.

"Yes, honey. But I think he might have appendicitis."

She was holding Sammy on her lap. The waiting room was bright, sectioned off with Plexiglas and furnished with green molded plastic seats. It was filled with people.

My mother had already pulled rank. We were next. The nurse stepped into the room, reading from a clipboard.

"Samuel Hoffman Weeks." She called Sammy's name just as my dad showed up. His hair was messy and he was sweating. He looked worried.

Sammy was sleeping again, with his head on my mother's lap.

Everything else happened pretty fast after that. A nurse took blood while Sammy screamed. The doctors talked to my parents. Then they took Sam into a room while my dad and I waited again in the waiting room. They had old TV sets bracketed onto the walls, all of them playing a different channel, but I didn't feel like moving.

For a long while I became completely engrossed in watching *Full House* in Spanish. I was surprised at how much I could understand, but maybe that was because I had seen that episode before.

"They need to get him to surgery," my mom said when she came out.

Sammy wasn't with her.

You Couldn't Pay Me Enough

"I am not going to her house," I said.

It was late. I was hungry. We had never gotten to eat. I was tired. And I was scared. My brother was going to have surgery. My parents didn't know how long it would take. They would be here overnight. And I couldn't stay.

"I've already called her," my mother was saying. "She's coming over in a cab to get you. And then you will spend the night at her house. I will call you in the morning. There is nothing I can do about it."

I still didn't understand. "Why can't I go to Nana and Poppy's? Why can't I?" But I knew she had already explained this. My grandfather wasn't home. He was down in Florida looking at condos.

"No," I was saying. "I'll stay here. I'll sleep on the chair. I'll stay up. Please. Please. Can't I stay at Rachel's? Can't you call her mom?"

Now I was begging.

"Caroline. I can't ask Sandi or Jay to drive all the way into the city now. Besides, it would take hours," my mother told me.

"I'll go to a hotel." I was crying. "Please, Daddy. Please."

My father hugged me. "Caroline, you're being a little over-dramatic. I know you're scared but Sam will be fine. We can't leave right now. It's important. Do you understand? We need you to do this for us. It's just one night."

How can you argue with that?

I nodded my head, and when my mother stepped toward us, I buried my head against her.

"It's okay, sweetie. I would know if it wasn't, right? It's okay. I'll owe you one for this, kiddo. For staying with New Aunt Gert. I'll owe you."

She'd better believe it.

Calèche

Being in New York City at night without my grandparents made me really sad. It was the darkness, the streetlights, the occasional clarity of voices, and the lonely sound of sirens in the distance. All the noises that used to remind me of visiting my nana, staying in her bedroom, breathing in her perfume, squished into the dip between two mattresses. And I missed her more than ever.

"Well, this is it," Aunt Gert told me.

Before we even got out of the cab a man in uniform, a blue uniform with gold tassels on the shoulders, came hurrying out of the apartment building to open the door for us.

"Mrs. Schwartz." He said it as a statement, like she might have forgotten who she was.

"Clyde. This is my grandniece, Caroline Weeks."

"Pleasure." The man tipped his hat to me.

Good God almighty.

The wind was much stronger here. I could tell by the way the cab door felt, braced against it. The wind seemed to race right up the block. When we stepped onto the street I could feel the cold right through my coat. My hair whipped around, wrapped around my face, and stayed there. Even when I tried to pull it from my eyes, another section of my hair took its place.

"I always wear a hat here," Aunt Gert said. "Riverside is the windiest part of the city."

"I don't mind," I said, but I was glad when we got inside. The walls were lined with mirrors, mirrors and marble. I made it a point not to look at myself as we walked to the elevators.

My new aunt Gert lived on the very top floor.

She *was* wearing a hat; I didn't even notice it till we got in the elevator. It had a feather on one side, and she was tall. Pretty tall for an old lady. Then my stomach growled really loudly just before the doors opened.

"I will get you something to eat," she said. "Right away."

I was embarrassed and grateful.

You could tell as soon as you walked into the apartment that never a child alive had stepped into this place. Well, maybe that was an exaggeration, but certainly no kid ever resided here. It was a museum. Untouchable. I watched as my aunt seemed to avoid stepping on her own rugs. They were tremendous, with intricate foreign-looking designs. Any piece of furniture that dared to stand on the rug had coasters under its feet.

Most everything was wood, dark wood. Shiny like it had just been cleaned an hour ago. There was even a stillness in the air, like nothing ever moved around in here. Or wasn't supposed to.

It didn't look anything like my grandparents' apartment.

The windows were draped in thick dark curtains ceiling to floor, and the places where the curtains were slightly parted, I could see another, lighter set of curtains behind them. I didn't know where to go.

"Let's go into the kitchen," Aunt Gert said. She was hanging up her coat in a hall closet and reaching out her hand to take mine.

"Thanks. I think I'll keep it," I said.

"Very well." She headed into another room, expecting me to follow. The kitchen, it wasn't anything like my nana's. This one was big, but the counters were mostly empty, and for some reason she had two refrigerators.

"How about some cottage cheese?" she asked me, opening one of them. "With a little cantaloupe. Oh, I don't have any. A sandwich?"

"Thanks," I answered.

She was awkward in the kitchen, with the bread and the slices of turkey. I wanted to offer to do it myself but I wasn't sure if that was ruder than just sitting here watching. When in doubt I usually choose to stick to what I was doing, which right now was nothing.

"Mayonnaise?"

"Yes, thank you."

Then there was the even more awkward moment when I realized I was the only one eating and that she would probably sit here and watch me. I was relieved when she put my plate down in front of me and said she was going into the spare room to see to my bedding.

But first she asked me, "Would you like something to drink?"

"Milk?" I thought that was a safe bet. Grown-ups usually like kids who drink milk. Besides, the younger I appeared, the less would be expected of me.

"I can't give you milk with your turkey sandwich. How about some juice? Orange?"

"That's fine. Thanks."

She poured the juice, left the room, and I was left sitting once again, wondering. Was this milk thing something like not traveling on Saturdays? A part of me knew it was. A part of me knew it was something Jewish. Not going to school on Yom Kippur. Lighting candles on Hanukkah, which we hadn't done in so long, the memory of it sat in my brain along with Barney the purple dinosaur, *Blue's Clues*, and circle time. Nana could have told me, I thought. Had I only asked.

I felt a shiver run through my whole body. I was tired and I was hungry.

I bit into my sandwich and finished my whole meal in about a minute. Juice and all. I was starving. Aunt Gert was still not back yet. My chair squeaked loudly across the floor as I pushed it from the table and got up.

Aunt Gert's living room, the one with the thick, dark drapes, is the biggest room, I figured, although I still hadn't seen the bedrooms down the hall. I needed to use a bathroom. There was a little door by the front hall. That must be it.

There was also a long, skinny wooden table against the far wall that seemed to have no other purpose than to sit huge ornate frames upon.

Yes, this was the bathroom. The kind nobody ever uses, with little shell-shaped soaps in a shell-shaped dish and plush hand towels with ribbon and an embroidered emblem right in the center that makes it hard to dry your hands with.

On my way out, I took a look at the photographs on the long table. I saw one that I was sure was my grandmother and grandfather, Nana and Poppy, but they were very young. The photo was black and white. It was a wedding photo.

It was so quiet in here, I could hear the ticking of the clock in the kitchen.

Why would she have this picture? I thought she hated my grandmother. I thought she was so opposed to the marriage, she never talked to her own brother again, until his wife died, my nana.

And is that how my nana and Poppy felt about my own father? I felt tears burning behind my eyes. Being in New York, being here at night, I missed my grandmother. I knew it couldn't be true.

And then suddenly I felt someone was behind me.

How had my aunt Gert sneaked up on me like that? So quietly I hadn't heard her walking down the hall? I spun around, but no one was there.

I looked back at the photos. This one must be my grandfather when he was young; I could just barely recognize him without his little rectangle moustache, but it was him. He was wearing a suit, his hands in his pockets, standing next to a tall young woman. Attractive but not pretty. She was wearing a huge, funny hat. She had her arms around him. It was his sister, it was my new aunt Gert before she got horribly ugly and mean. Or maybe she was mean then, too.

They looked like they loved each other. There was even a little photo, a color one in the back, in a more modern-looking frame. It was my family, a long time ago. Me and Sam and my mom and dad. I barely remembered when we took it. On vacation in

Nora Raleigh Baskin

Florida visiting my dad's mom just before she died. I was about six years old. Sam was a newborn. How did she get this?

Just then the phone rang down the hall. I heard Aunt Gert's muffled voice. I hoped it was my parents calling to tell me everything was all right. Sam was fine and they were coming to get me and we'd all go home.

"Caroline?"

I stepped toward the hall. "Yeah?"

"Can you pick up the phone in the kitchen? Your mother wants to speak with you."

"Okay."

I nearly banged into the wall as I turned and headed back toward the kitchen. I had turned out the light after putting my dish and glass in the sink. I tried to scan the dark room with my eyes wide as could be, looking for the phone as I felt around the wall for the light switch.

My hand moved up and down as my eyes adjusted to the darkness. Edges of the counter, the stove, the refrigerator became clearer. *I think that's the phone over by that calendar.* I didn't want to wait to turn on the light. As I made my way through the shadows and across the floor, I felt something brush by me. I felt something warm, something beside me, and I stopped when I smelled something familiar, like perfume.

Nana?

"Caroline?" my aunt called out again. "Can you find the phone?"

As quickly as it had come, the perfume was gone. I picked up the phone and spoke with my parents.

Sammy had his operation. He was fine. He was in recovery but my parents didn't want to leave the hospital. They would stay there all night. They had a little chair-bed set up in Sammy's room.

No, no. I was fine. Don't worry. Of course, I'd see them in the morning.

I love you, too. Both of you.

I will.

Bye.

I'll Always Be with You

Was it really only six months ago? That last visit with Nana and Poppy. Gold's Deli. Chocolate egg creams. The pickles and the doctor's appointment. And me walking behind my grandmother, pretending I didn't know who she was.

Poppy was taking me and Sammy to Grand Central Station to meet our dad and to catch a train back home. It was time for us to go home.

Nana insisted on coming downstairs to say good-bye even though she hadn't put on her makeup. No foundation, no fake eyelashes, not even her eyebrows. She didn't outline with pencil, but she ran her red lipstick over her lips without even looking in the mirror.

"What?" she said. "I know where my lips are."

I should have known then.

"But, Nana," I told her. "You never leave the house without your face."

"Who needs to put on a face?" she said. "When I have my two grandchildren."

When we walked outside, the sun was shining bright. It was spring. The light fell across the tall buildings and landed only on our side of the street. My grandfather walked to the curb and lifted his hand to hail a cab. Nana and I waited outside the lobby. I thought she looked younger without her makeup, softer. More like my mother.

"It's beautiful, isn't it?" my grandmother said. "The world is beautiful."

"Nana, why are you crying?" I asked her.

"I don't know. Sometimes I miss people. I miss my mother."

I had never heard my grandmother speak like that. The stories she told about her life, about her family, always sounded like stories. Like books at a far end of the shelf, not real. I had never heard my grandmother sound as she did now, like a little girl.

Like me.

I suddenly turned and wrapped my arms around her waist.

"I'm so sorry, Nana," I said.

"For what, Caroline? You haven't done anything."

"For what I did yesterday coming back from the doctor. When I didn't answer you. When I walked behind you." I shrugged my shoulders like it was no big deal, but I was scared. I had let her walk too far ahead.

"I just wanted to pretend I was by myself. I didn't mean to hurt your feelings."

Suddenly she laughed. She hadn't laughed all weekend. "Oh, my *shayna maideleh*, that's what children do. That's what they're supposed to do, grow up. Move away. Go out on their own, test the waters . . . all that kind of thing."

I reached up and took her hand. "I don't want to go out on my own, Nana." I told her.

"Not to worry," she told me, squeezing my hand. "You will always be my *shayna madel*."

Sammy was shouting to me. They were waiting for me, the cab door was open. Sammy was already inside.

"And I will always be with you," my nana told me. "Even when we are apart."

The Truth Comes Out

"You're surprised to see that photograph here, aren't you?" asked Aunt Gert.

After I hung up with my parents and they told me Sammy was okay, I realized I was still holding my grandparents' wedding photo in my hands. My aunt Gert had come into the kitchen and turned on the light.

"A little," I said. There didn't seem to be much use in lying.

"I love my brother very much, Caroline. I loved your grandmother, too. Things aren't always how they sound. Sometimes they sound worse when they are taken out of context. I think a lot of life's problems are just misunderstandings no one bothers to fix."

I suppose that was true. I thought about my invitation to Lauren's party. I thought about walking behind my grandmother just so I could pretend to be older. What if I had never talked about either of those things, to anyone?

"Come, let's sit down for a minute," Aunt Gert said. She gestured toward a sitting room off the living room. A room that actually looked like someone had used it. There were books and newspapers, a coffee table with a pair of glasses on top. Comfortable-looking, sat-in-looking upholstered chairs in which I sat, and as soon as I did, my back ached and I needed to lean back. My head plopped back on the cushions without asking my permission.

"You're tired," Aunt Gert said. "Would you like to see where you are going to sleep? There is a bathroom in there as well. I laid out towels and an extra brand-new toothbrush."

"No, I'm fine," I said. I wanted to know what she knew. I put the photo down on the coffee table and my aunt Gert picked it up.

"Our father was a very severe man, Caroline." She ran her fingers across the glass in the frame. "He had worked hard his whole life. He was especially hard on his son, your grandfather. He was not a very loving father. He demanded respect."

I thought about my mother. She was hard on me, all the time. But I knew she loved me. I never doubted that.

"I should have been married by then, I was older, but, well . . . I was not particularly pretty. It's hard to explain. My father let me know this almost daily. Men made money and women were pretty. I was never going to get married, so he put all his efforts into his seventeen-year-old son, your grandfather. He wanted his son to marry this young woman, Rita Gordon, I remember, the daughter of one of his business associates."

As I watched my aunt Gert talking I could see something in her face, almost a version of her younger self. Not beautiful, but strong. What she must have looked like without the wrinkles and the spots. Handsome, the kind of woman they call handsome. Which, I hope, is never me.

She went on. "But my brother was in love. He wasn't going to marry so young, but, well, his father forced his hand. When your grandparents ran off and got married at town hall in Brooklyn, my father was furious. He cut off your grandfather in every way. He threatened to make my mother sit shivah. I had never seen a woman cry so much."

"Shivah? Isn't that when someone dies?"

"Yes, the mourning period," Aunt Gert told me. "Mourners sit on boxes so they can't be too comfortable. They cover their mirrors so they won't be vain."

I remembered the mirrors at my grandparent's apartment draped in sheets. I couldn't imagine doing that just because your son didn't do what you wanted him to do.

"But I thought your family *wasn't* religious. I thought they hated my grandmother because she was too Jewish?"

Aunt Gert took in a deep breath and let it out slowly. "That was partly it. Not the religion but the class, maybe. Your grandmother—Nana, right? You called her Nana?"

I nodded.

"Your nana was an eastern European Jew, from Russia. Her mother was born there, in Lbov, I believe. My family had been in the country for three generations already, from Germany. My family didn't speak with an accent. We never spoke Yiddish. We even had a Christmas tree. We had done pretty much everything we could not to *look* Jewish."

Looking Jewish? Like the little boy I saw at the Bronx Zoo with the black hat and the curls of hair? Like getting to mail out bat mitzvah invitations? Like me wearing my Star of David necklace? Being Jewish but not sure I wanted anyone to know?

Nora Raleigh Baskin

"It was hard," Aunt Gert went on. "I don't blame them really. A Jew couldn't make it in the business world. Door were shut to us. Clubs, organizations. Colleges."

"Colleges?"

"Oh, yes. Colleges. Certain towns, even." Aunt Gert seemed to be talking to herself almost, figuring it all out. When the sadness took over her face, instead of the meanness, she looked almost pretty.

"So my family just kept their Judaism to themselves. Hoffman is a German name. It didn't have to be Jewish. We were Jewish; we just didn't wear our Judaism on our sleeves."

Being Jewish came at certain cost. But I already knew that, didn't I? Even before I understood, I had felt it. From Lauren. From Rachel. From the Orthodox boy with the blue eyes. From my grandparents.

And from myself.

"After my brother defied our father and left home, I was more afraid. I was afraid I would be alone forever. I was afraid I would never marry and if I upset my father I would have no one. So I did what he asked. I didn't talk to my brother or his wife."

"Ever again? How did you get those pictures?"

She smiled. "Well, we spoke when we could."

"Did you . . . ," I began. "Did you ever get married? Do you have any kids?"

At this Aunt Gert smiled again. "Yes," she told me. "I fell in love. I was much older. Our father had passed away. I married my husband and we had eighteen wonderful years. And you know the funny thing?"

Could anything about this be funny? "What?" I asked.

"After all that controversy with your nana's family, I married a very observant Jewish man. We kept a kosher home. I became *shomer shabbos*."

I had no idea what that meant.

Aunt Gert went on. "We weren't blessed with any children; I was too old. But we had love."

I heard her make a little sound, almost a sob, but she swallowed it away.

"My husband was my great love," she told me. "I was a very lucky woman. And now I am lucky to know you."

I Am a Bat Mitzvah

My aunt Gert didn't get out of the cab when we got to the hospital where we were meeting my parents. I think it was hard for her to get up and down. She waved at my father and I watched as she leaned forward and spoke to the driver. I watched still, as the yellow car pulled around the circle and into traffic.

The sunshine was taking up most of the world. Even though it was cold, it was clear and bright. It was November, and the snowflakes started to fall. One by one at first, almost as if someone were throwing them from a rooftop, then all at once. The tiny ones that drift and float around right in front of you before they land.

My dad would drive me home and pick up some fresh clothes. Sam was fine but my mother wanted to stay with him. My dad would go back in the afternoon and I could stay at Rachel's.

"Daddy?"

"Yes, sweetie?"

"Nothing."

We drove back, this time with the Hudson River on our left side. The snow had stopped but it was getting grayer out. Colder.

"Are you taking me right to Rachel's or are we going home first?"

"Home first," he said.

"Good."

We were silent for a time. It was always comfortable not to say anything with my dad. I never felt like he was angry if I wasn't talking. After a long while I said, "Good, because I need to get something first."

Of course, sometimes I wished he would talk a little more.

"I need to get something important."

"What? What, sweetie? What do you need?"

He was probably thinking about Sam. He was probably really tired. He probably hadn't slept much, if at all.

"I need to get my Jewish star necklace." There, I said it. "The one that Nana left for me. She wanted me to have it."

"Oh, yes. I know. I haven't seen you wear it."

"You know? You know I have it? How do you know?"

My dad shifted gears. He checked his mirrors and changed lanes. "Your grandfather told me about it. He told me he gave it to you. Did you lose it, sweetie? Are you upset?"

"No, I just thought . . . I don't know." I was quiet again.

"You thought I'd mind," my dad said. "You thought if you wore your Jewish star that it would be disloyal to me because I'm not Jewish, right?"

"Something like that."

I liked riding in the car because I could look straight ahead. I

Nora Raleigh Baskin

didn't have to show my face or look at someone else's. I could just talk and just listen. But nobody could leave, nobody could go anywhere.

We were buckled in.

"Caroline. I married your mother. I love everything about her. I love that she is Jewish. You can be and do anything you want."

I raised my eyebrows at him. "Anything?"

"You know what I mean, wise guy."

"But what about Mom?" I asked.

"What about her?"

"Would she care if I was wearing Nana's necklace? Wouldn't she think I was being silly?"

"Silly?"

I waited, and then I said, "You know, because of the car. Because her mother and father didn't want you two to get married in the first place."

I had never seen my dad laugh so hard, which was kind of good, since he'd looked so beat and tired a few minutes ago.

"Where did you hear that?" he wanted to know.

"Mom."

"*She* told you that?"

I nodded. "She said it hurt your feelings."

"Well, yes and no," my father said, and then he told me another love story.

This one was about a young Jewish girl in medical school, a young resident whose parents didn't want her to get married. Not yet. And yes, probably they would have rather she married a Jewish man. And yes, they offered to buy her a car if she waited. But my father had won them over with his infinite charms.

Besides, he was clearly crazy about their daughter.

And yes, there was mention of a car. A BMW? Was it?

My dad thought it had been a Jaguar. "Now, a Jaguar she might have thought twice about."

"Da-ad." I hit him on the arm.

It wasn't for another half an hour, until we crossed the border into Connecticut and we were almost home, that I spoke again.

"I know I don't need to have one to be Jewish, but *could* I? Could I have a bat mitzvah if I wanted?"

"Yes," my dad said. "You can have a bat mitzvah if you want to."

I knew my dad would tell my mother about what I said, about me wanting a bat mitzvah. I think I probably wanted him to. She wasn't mad at all. In fact, we started talking more about Nana and about all things Jewish. I told her about the stuff Aunt Gert told me about bat mitzvahs and bar mitzvahs, and my mom told me some stuff too.

"You know, Caroline," my mom said to me. We were alone, sitting on the couch. Our favorite doctor love-show was on but there was a commercial.

"What?" I asked.

"Well, I'm going to tell you."

"Okay, but our show is going to be on soon."

My feet were resting on my mother's legs, and her feet were almost touching my chin, but I didn't mind.

"In the Jewish religion, some people believe that the dead are not really gone. That they watch over us. Take care of the ones they loved. During certain holidays there is a special memorial service in synagogue for them. Very religious Jews believe that our loved ones actually come down into the sanctuary and look for the people who are saying a prayer for them."

"Like what holiday?"

"Like Yom Kippur," she told me. Our show was coming on but I turned toward her.

"Really? I thought you didn't believe in stuff like that."

"When did I say that?" she asked.

I decided not to pursue that one.

My mother went on. "I always thought you could be with someone you loved whenever you want."

"You do?" I asked. "Like when?"

"Like whenever you remember them," she told me.

I think I understood now.

People become memories but they are still there. They are there to grab on to when you are swimming in the ocean, when you dream that you are drowning. We are all like the links on my chain. Something to connect us to everyone who came before.

And everyone who will come after.

34

All Things That Go Around

Today was make-up day for pictures. There was only a handful of us here in the library—everybody who'd missed getting their picture taken for one reason or another. Being absent, getting to school late, or crawling around on your hands and knees when your name was called.

Stuff like that.

"Hey, Caroline." It was a girl from my science class, Joanne Parkhill.

"Hey, Joanne."

The photographer was setting up his backdrop again, adjusting his tripod. There was no box of combs today that I could see.

"I missed picture day," Joanne told me.

"I figured," I said. Then, in case that sounded too sarcastic, I added, "Me, too."

"But you don't get to be in your class photo. They're not going to get your whole class in here again and just take a whole other class photo just because you missed photo day. Right? I mean that would be dumb, right?"

"Right."

"Why did you miss picture day? I was out sick. I had this thing called Coxsackie virus . . . but it's not as bad as it sounds. It's like chicken pox, but you only get it on your hands and feet. Isn't that strange?"

Joanne does this in science class, too. That's why the teacher never calls on her even though she has her hand up every time. She always has the right answer; it's just that she can't stop talking.

But she's really good in science and she's not a bad kid. I kinda like her.

There were no bleachers set up this time. No lines outside the library. It all felt pretty civilized, actually. The photographer looked much more relaxed. I reached up and touched my necklace. I moved the star back and forth along the chain carefully, but I knew it was safe. It wouldn't break again.

Not only because I was going to be more careful, but also because my mom bought me a thicker chain, real gold, with a stronger clasp. It was an early birthday present.

"Joanne Parkhill. Is Joanne Parkhill here?"

"Okeydokcy. Here goes," Joanne said to me. "See ya later, Caroline."

I waved to her and then, when I turned around, I saw Ryan.

"You missed picture day too?" Ryan said to me.

"Well, not really."

I kind of wanted to tell him. I mean, he picked me to be on his volleyball team the other day. He's really nice, actually.

"What do you mean?" he asked me.

"Well, I was here, but I didn't get my picture taken."

"Oh, my mom's making me do a retake 'cause my eyes were closed," Ryan said.

Most everyone here was on the other side of the room by the photographer, waiting their turn. Ryan and I were standing by the computers. He was leaning against one of the tables.

I wasn't sure what to do, where to look. If they called my name I'd just wave and say see ya later. If they called him first, I'd still wave, and I'd still say see ya later.

"I like your necklace," Ryan said to me.

I reached my hand up. "Oh, thanks. It was my grandmother's. She wanted me to have it."

"So you're Jewish?"

Yes, I am.

And in another month I will be thirteen years old, I thought to myself. I will be a bat mitzvah whether we mark the occasion or not. Which I might do, but I might not. But I wanted to wear this necklace for my school photo.

It's like a mini bat mitzvah celebration. A statement I am making to the world. The start of a commitment. A gift I am just about ready to open.

"Yeah," I said. "I'm Jewish."

To this Ryan lifted his chin a little, in a nodding gesture. His body hadn't moved at all. He was still leaning against the computer table. His legs stretched out, his feet crossed.

"I didn't know that," he told me. "I didn't know you were Jewish."

I was about to brace myself, but something told me this time was different. I relaxed. I didn't say anything.

"So am I," Ryan said.

And I just smiled.

Nora Raleigh Baskin

35

Like Links on a Chain

There is a five-piece orchestra and a female vocalist in a sequined gown. People are already dancing when we walk into the room. There are lavender tablecloths and baskets of African violets blooming in tiny purple blossoms on every table.

I am full from eating all the food that has been walking around during the cocktail hour—teriyaki chicken on skewers, cocktail hot dogs, and guess what? *Knishes!* Little doughy things stuffed with potato goo.

And Ryan Berk is here. Because when Rachel invited Lauren, we got to invite one more boy, so Rachel invited him. She did that for me. Ryan really is a good dancer, especially when we don't have to do a hoedown. I think he's waiting for a slow dance so he can ask me again. He hasn't asked Lauren once.

But Rachel—Rachel is amazing.

I think I understand it better now.

At the service, there were people from all over, people from all parts of Rachel's life and her family's lives. There were family and friends, the rabbi and just people from their congregation, neighbors and kids from school. And there was Rachel telling us all that she is Jewish and wants to stay that way. She stood in front of everyone in that synagogue, those known to her and those who were strangers, and she wore her Judaism right there on her sleeve.

Her voice was shaking at first. But it got stronger the more she sang and chanted. When she caught my eye, I smiled at her. I think it helped.

But not everything here at the party is going as planned. Rachel's mom looks pretty nervous. I know there is some major confusion with the food or the wine, something that isn't right, or isn't there, or there isn't enough of. But no one else would have noticed.

Rachel, in her white socked feet (all the girls got socks to put on over their stockings for when they can't stand their high heels one minute longer) comes running across the lobby floor just as I am coming out of the bathroom.

"What's wrong?" I ask.

"Oh, nothing. My mom wanted me to tell the caterer guy something. All done. I was just getting back to the party."

"Rachel," I say to her. "You look so beautiful. You did a great job, a wonderful job, at your service. You made me cry."

Even though she had stopped running before, now Rachel pauses. She puts her hands on my shoulders. "That means so much to me, Caroline. I was so scared. You're the only one who knows that."

"But you did it," I say.

She smiles so big her cheeks are touching her eyes. "I'm glad it's over."

Nora Raleigh Baskin

"And even with Lauren here, your party is fantastic," I say. "Everyone is having so much fun."

"Are you?" she asks.

"Me?"

"Well, I mean . . . you don't feel bad, do you? Because you wanted one?"

"I am one, Rachel. I mean, I will be on my birthday next month."

It is just the two of us; the doors to the social hall are closed. We can hear the music swelling, the clarinets and trumpets. The voice of the singer. We can hear all the happy voices mixing together, creating a kind of music of their own. It is cacophonous and wonderful.

But we stand alone together in the center of this huge lobby. Two small dots, two girls. Two best friends, separated at birth.

"What do you mean?" Rachel asks.

"Because I *am* Jewish. Because my mother is Jewish, I became a bat mitzvah when I turned twelve. Automatically. I don't have to do anything. Just be me. My aunt Gert told me that."

Just then the doors fly open and Sandi Miller pokes her head out.

"Rachel! Caroline! Come quick. The hora. It's time for the hora!" Her face is flushed and her makeup is running, and her hair is already coming out of her upsweep, but I have never seen her look prettier, happier. More excited.

"Coming, Mom," Rachel says. She turns back to me. "You're kidding. Is that true? I did all this work and studying and I didn't have to?"

I smile and shake my head. "Nope."

But I know it was all worth it and so does she. It is the happiest day of her life. Her life so far.

"You *are* a bat mitzvah, Rachel. Just because you're Jewish," I say.

"*Now* you tell me!" Rachel shouts.

We link arms and together we run back inside, to eat and dance, and to celebrate who we are.

Glossary

bar mitzvah: a Jewish boy who has reached the age of thirteen, who is now obligated as an adult member of the community to obey the "mitzvoth" (commandments). One does not "have" a bar mitzvah, one becomes a bar mitzvah. Literally means "son of the commandment."

bat mitzvah: a Jewish girl who has reached the age where she is now obligated as an adult member of the community to obey the "mitzvoth" (commandments). In traditional Judaism, this happens at age twelve, but more liberal circles have set the age at thirteen. One does not "have" a bat mitzvah, one becomes a bat mitzvah. Literally means "daughter of the commandment."

dreidel: a spinning top with four sides, played as a game on Hanukkah. Each side of the dreidel has a Hebrew letter, which creates an acronym, translated from Hebrew as "a great miracle happened there."

keep kosher: to observe the laws of the Torah and its rabbinic interpreters concerning what foods are permissible to eat.

knish: an eastern European food. A knish, round or rectangular in shape, consists of a filling (usually potato or meat), covered by dough, which is then baked or fried.

menorah: the seven-branched candelabra that stood in the ancient holy temple in Jerusalem. Now, the word is how most people refer to a *chanukiyah*, the nine-branched candelabra used to celebrate the eight days of Hanukkah.

oy vey: Yiddish expression of concern, translated as "woe is me."

peyes: the uncut and unshaven sideburns of religious Jewish men who are following a commandment in the Torah.

Rosh Hashanah: literally, "head of the year." This is the holiday marking the Jewish new year. This day begins the ten days of repentance, when Jews ask for forgiveness from those whom they have wronged. Customs of the holiday include attending prayer services, hearing the sound of the shofar (the ram's horn), and eating apples dipped in honey to symbolize a sweet new year.

shayna maideleh: Yiddish for "beautiful girl."

shivah: the period of intense mourning after the death of a close relative. Shivah traditionally lasts seven days.

shomer shabbos: one who observes the prohibitions against any type of work on the Sabbath, which particularly includes lighting fires. In modern days, one who is shomer shabbos does not use electricity.

yarmulkes (or *yarmulkas*, or *kippot*): head coverings traditionally worn by men during a Jewish prayer service. They symbolize how Jews are always watched over by God (though some would say they symbolize that God is always above them).

Yom Kippur: literally, "the day of atonement." Observed on the tenth day of the new year; its customs include fasting and praying in atonement for one's sins, and seeking forgiveness from God. It is the most serious and solemn day in the Jewish year.